RED ROCK MYSTERIES

#1 BEST-SELLING AUTHORS

JERRY B. JENKINS · CHRIS FABRY

Visit Tyndale's exciting Web site for kids at cool2read.com
Also see the Web site for adults at tyndale.com

*TYNDALE* is a registered trademark of Tyndale House Publishers, Inc.
*Tyndale Kids* logo is a trademark of Tyndale House Publishers, Inc.

*Wind Chill*
Copyright © 2006 by Jerry B. Jenkins. All rights reserved.

Cover and interior photographs copyright © 2004 by Brian MacDonald. All rights reserved.

Authors' photograph © 2004 by Brian MacDonald. All rights reserved.

Designed by Jacqueline L. Noe
Edited by Lorie Popp

Published in association with the literary agency of Alive Communications, Inc., 7680 Goddard Street, Suite 200, Colorado Springs, CO 80920.

Scripture quotations are taken from the *Holy Bible,* New Living Translation, copyright © 1996, 2004. Used by permission of Tyndale House Publishers, Inc., Carol Stream, Illinois 60188. All rights reserved.

**Library of Congress Cataloging-in-Publication Data**

Jenkins, Jerry B.
    Wind chill / Jerry B. Jenkins, Chris Fabry.
      p. cm. — (Tyndale kids) (Red rock mysteries ; 14)
    Summary: While participating in a forensics contest, twins Ashley and Bryce investigate not only the disappearance of a college student but also behind-the-scenes dirty tricks during the public speaking competition.
    ISBN-13: 978-1-4143-0153-2 (sc : alk. paper)
    ISBN-10: 1-4143-0153-7 (sc : alk. paper)
    [1. Forensics (Public speaking)—Fiction.    2. Christian life—Fiction.    3. Twins—Fiction.
4. Brothers and sisters—Fiction.    5. Colorado—Fiction.    6. Mystery and detective stories.]
I. Fabry, Chris, date.    II. Title.    III. Series.    IV. Series: Jenkins, Jerry B. Red rock mysteries ; 14.

PZ7.J4138Wid 2006
[Fic]—dc22                                                                                    2006013825

Printed in the United States of America

09    08    07    06
9    8    7    6    5    4    3    2    1

Ingram 04/24/08  5.99

WIND CHILL

# WIND CHILL

**14**

TYNDALE HOUSE PUBLISHERS, INC., CAROL STREAM, ILLINOIS

*To Brandi Ring*

"Commit a **crime** and the earth is made of glass. Commit a crime, and it seems as if a coat of snow fell on the ground, such as reveals in the woods the track of every partridge, and fox, and squirrel."

Ralph Waldo Emerson

"Whose **woods** these are I think I know. His house is in the village though; He will not see me stopping here To watch the woods fill up with snow."

Robert Frost

"To appreciate the **beauty** of a snowflake, it is necessary to stand out in the cold."

Anonymous

PART 1

# CHAPTER 1

✖ Ashley ✖

Hayley Henderson and Marion Quidley huddled with me in the Penrose Middle School auditorium as we awaited the final results of our forensics tournament. *Forensics* is just a fancy word for "speech."

My twin, Bryce, competes in Oral Interpretation of Humor. His routine, "Good Morning, Baghdad," is hysterical, and he's the best at the tournament. He told me that he'd nailed his last performance.

I compete in Solo Acting. Bryce and I tried Duet Humor last year, and that was a disaster. It was easy to practice with each other, but we learned there are some things we shouldn't try. Most of the year I thought he was competing in the Irritate Ashley competition, winning first place each time.

The eight finalists in Bryce's category were onstage, accepting awards. It was down to Bryce and a kid with a goofy smile. Sometimes the way you look can mean all the difference in the humor category.

Marion has a thing for Bryce, and she couldn't stop jumping. "He's going to do it, Ashley! He's really going to do it!"

The announcer, a blonde woman with a lot of energy, took her time. "And first place . . . in Oral Interpretation of Humor . . . goes to . . . Red Rock's Bryce Timberline!"

All the Red Rock kids squealed, even me. Bryce held up the trophy and waved. Marion swooned like he was some rock star.

Next up was Impromptu, Marion's event. In that competition you're given a topic, and you have to make up a speech to support your views. Marion is really smart, and she blows away the competition when she gets a good topic. It's like watching a six-foot-five-inch high school kid play middle school basketball. No *uh*s or *um*s from this girl. She frames her argument logically, supports it with facts, and usually ends with a killer summary. I think she'll make a good lawyer.

Bryce joined us, holding on to his trophy like it was real gold.

When Marion's name was called for first place, we all went wild. It was kind of sad because Marion's mom and dad hadn't been to one competition, but the rest of us yelled even louder.

Hayley got sixth place in her event, and her shoulders slumped. I hugged her, and she tried to act like she didn't care, but I could read her face.

They called my category, and I walked onstage. One of the other contestants had performed a scene based on *The Diary of Anne Frank*, and just about everybody in the room cried. I hoped I didn't get eighth place.

# CHAPTER 2

### ☺ Bryce ☺

*Life is a series of wins and losses.* At least that's what our coach, Mr. Gminski, says. He tells us to do our best, forget our mistakes, and see what happens. That's exactly what Ashley had done the whole year. She's the most competitive girl I know—evidenced by the way she gritted her teeth and held her breath as each name was called. Our group screamed and pumped our fists; then things got deathly quiet. It's a lot easier being onstage than being a spectator.

In the end, Ashley got second place, and Hayley and Marion would have put her on their shoulders if they could have caught her. She hopped around the auditorium like a kangaroo after a Starbucks binge.

The other team members who did well were Kael Barnes and Lynette Jarvis. They won first in Duet Humor. It was easy to congratulate Kael, because he's my friend, but Lynette is a different story. Ever since she moved here at the beginning of the school year, she's been a pain. She used to live in Wyoming, and let's just say I've been a burr under her saddle. To make matters worse, she's the prettiest cowgirl this side of the Mississippi, if you know what I mean.

The awards ceremony ended, and Mr. Gminski lined our team up onstage. It just happened that I stood beside Lynette. "Good job," I said.

She looked at me like I was a horse dropping and moved to the end of the line.

Marion took her place, smiling at me like I was her favorite horse. "Good job," she said.

It's funny how life will do that. Someone you like snubs you; then someone you don't care for looks at you starry-eyed and you want to leave. "Thanks. You too," I said.

"Your routine is really funny," she continued. "Everybody was talking about how perfect the material is. . . ."

I like attention, but Marion talked as Mr. Gminski snapped the photo. Later I grabbed the digital camera and saw that everyone was looking at the camera but Marion and me. We were staring at each other. It took everything in me not to erase the picture.

A judge found Mr. Gminski and took him to a room filled with coaches.

"I'll bet somebody got disqualified," Marion said. "They never do that after the awards are handed out unless there's a protest."

People whispered, and wild rumors flew around the auditorium. Since I'm Mr. Gminski's aide, I had a clue about what was up.

The blonde lady with the big voice hurried to the microphone and told everyone to sit. "We have some exciting news. As some of you know, RMIFT"—she pronounced it R-miffed—"has established a competition this year for . . ." She must have seen the looks on everybody's faces because she said, "It's the Rocky Mountain Invitational Forensics Tournament. Those who qualify will compete with other top finishers in Colorado, Wyoming, and New Mexico."

"Have you heard about this?" Ashley whispered. When I didn't say anything right away, she snarled at me.

"Mr. Gminski said there might be another tournament, but—"

"The good news is," the blonde lady said, "after tabulating the year-end scores, several of you have made the cut for RMIFT. Here's the list."

Each time she read a name, a group celebrated. When they called my name, I held up my trophy and pumped my fist. Ashley, Marion, Kael, and Lynette were also called. The other team members were happy for us, but I could tell they felt left out.

**CHAPTER 3**

❀ Ashley ❀

"What does it mean?" one kid yelled after all the names were called. It was the question we were all asking.

The woman held up her hands to quiet us. "RMIFT is being held at CSD and—"

"What's CSD?" someone asked.

I love it when grown-ups use acronyms. Makes me feel better because I use so many.

"Colorado School of Drama," she said. "It's in Tres Peaks, near Rocky Mountain National Park."

I looked at Bryce. Tres Peaks (Three Peaks) was one of our favorite

places in any season. In winter it has great skiing, tubing, and snow-
boarding, and it's not as crowded as Breckenridge or some of the
other ski areas. In the summer, Tres Peaks is cooler than where we
live because it sits at more than 11,000 feet. Sometimes Sam takes us
camping in the national park, and it feels like we're a million miles
from everyone. The stars are bright at night, elk and deer run free, and
the small town has lots of gift shops.

"If you're invited," the woman said, "you'll stay Thursday to
Sunday competing. There will probably be some time for skiing and
other winter sports, depending on the weather."

Bryce looked at Kael, and they gave each other a high five.

"The school will be on break that week," the lady continued, "so
you'll stay in the dorms, eat lunch in their cafeteria—"

"Two days off school, plus skiing?" Bryce whispered. "I'm there!"

"—and the winners of that competition will go to the western finals in Hollywood."

My heart did a backflip, then a double somersault with a twist,
and stuck its landing. I'd wanted to be an actress for so long, and I'd
heard about CSD. It was my first choice for a college, even though
that was four years away. But a trip to Hollywood seemed too good
to be true.

"How much will it cost?" Marion shouted.

"There's a fee for entrance to the competition and meals," the
lady said. "I think it's $175."

Marion's face fell. Marion was long on talent but short on money.
Her dad had been hurt in an accident, and her mom was barely
keeping the family going.

I put an arm around her. "We'll figure out some way to get you
there," I said.

She nodded, but I don't think she believed me.

When we got on the bus to go home, Hayley sat with someone else instead of with me. If you want to know the definition of a bittersweet victory, it's what I experienced that day.

# CHAPTER 4

☻ *Bryce* ☻

*When the forensics team travels,* we usually stop at Wendy's and pay for our own food, but once a year Mr. Gminski and some teachers pitch in and pay for our dinner at The Silver Plate. It's one of those all-you-can-eat places where you can get filet mignon or corn dogs, baked salmon or fish sticks.

I felt bad for those who hadn't made RMIFT but excited for the rest of us. The money didn't bother me because I knew Mom and Sam would pay. (We call him Sam because he's our stepdad, not our real dad.) Ashley and I would probably babysit Dylan, our little brother, and do extra chores, so I didn't expect a problem.

Mr. Gminski raised a plastic cup of Diet Coke and saluted the whole team. (It makes me laugh when grown-ups with round bellies fill their plates and then drink Diet Coke.) He gave out awards like Comeback Player, Encourager of the Year, and dumb certificates too. I got the Best Run for the Bathroom award for an incident I'd rather not see in print. Trust me, we were all laughing when he finished.

I grabbed one more blueberry muffin and some baked fish at the buffet, then spotted Lynette on the way back to my seat. Her plate just had some fruit and vegetables on it. I thought about walking past her and not saying anything, but I couldn't. "You think there will be anyone from your old school at RMIFT?"

She glanced up, crunching a stalk of celery like it was my neck. "I doubt it."

"Be kind of neat if there was, don't you think?"

*Crunch. Crunch.* "Sure." She looked at her plate, which was almost empty. I can see studying a plate with country-fried steak or sweet-and-sour shrimp and egg rolls, but you don't study bits of carrots and broccoli unless you don't want to talk to the person in front of you.

"You and Kael really did great this year," I said. "Some kids work all three years of middle school, and you guys just started before Christmas, right?"

*Crunch. Crunch.* She nodded.

I looked at my muffin, which suddenly didn't seem half as appetizing as it had under the warm buffet lights. The baked fish turned soggy, and my tartar sauce ran on the hot plate. Wow. Now she had *me* studying food. "Do you like to ski?" I said.

She dropped a piece of broccoli and stared at me. "Look, Timberline, you don't have to try to be nice. I know how you feel. You know how I feel. My mom told you not to badger me."

"Badger?" I said. "I was just—"

"Drop it!" she said so loud that everybody in the restaurant looked at us. Then she lowered her voice. "Leave me alone. I don't like you; you don't like me. That's how it is. Okay?"

I nodded and walked away, bumping into Kael. "What was that all about?" he said.

I shook my head and retreated to my table, where Marion was waiting. She handed me a full glass of Mountain Dew mixed with Dr Pepper. "I brought a refill," she said. "It's what you like, right?"

I wanted to ask her to leave me alone, but I set the drink by my cold fish and tepid muffin. It had just the right amount of ice, and Marion had put the Dr Pepper on the bottom, the way I like it.

"Thanks," I said.

# CHAPTER 5

❋ Ashley ❋

When Mr. Gminski finished his meal, I asked how I'd made it to the tournament.

"You had enough first and second finishes to qualify," he said. "But the competition gets a lot tougher at RMIFT."

"What about Hayley?"

He winced. "She was really close. If she'd have finished third or better, she'd be going."

I tried to talk with Hayley, but she was in a corner booth with a cell phone to her ear, looking out at Pikes Peak, all purple and red in the twilight. I don't know about you, but I've been in that booth before.

I ate an ice-cream sundae until my stomach was so full I didn't think I could squeeze onto the bus.

When we filed into the parking lot, a car zoomed up. It was Mrs. Henderson. Hayley jumped inside. The whole thing put a damper on our celebration.

I got on the bus and sat behind Lynette. I'd heard her tiff with Bryce and wondered if she'd even look at me. "Congratulations," I said. "You and Kael should do well at the tournament."

"Yeah, you too. I think your performance has gotten better every week."

Hmm. She sure wasn't treating me like she treated Bryce. I leaned forward. "You were fighting with my brother in there. He can be a pain."

She shook her head. "He gets on my nerves. Tell him I didn't mean to yell."

Marion was the last person to get on the bus, and she sat by me. Her head was down, and she wiped her eyes.

"What's wrong?" I said.

"I called my mom and told her. She said there's no way we can afford this."

# CHAPTER 6

◎ *Bryce* ◎

**Mom and Sam beamed** and Dylan squealed when we told them about the trip. Dylan had no idea what we were talking about, but that didn't stop him from hopping around the house. Leigh, our older stepsister, was so thrilled that she said, "Huh" and went to the kitchen.

"Mr. Gminski sent an e-mail to parents, but I never expected both of you!" Mom said. "Do they need chaperones?"

I stared at Ashley. The last thing we wanted was for our mother to spoil the best trip of eighth grade. "He didn't say anything about . . ."

"No," Ashley said quickly. "I'm sure they have that covered."

Later Ashley told me what Lynette had said on the bus, and I just shook my head. "I'm staying out of her way from now until the end of time."

"You're going to avoid her?"

"She hates my guts and everything else about me."

I closed the door to my room and put the trophy on the dresser. I kept looking at it, picturing the trophy from RMIFT. It would be as big as my dresser. I jumped in bed and couldn't help smiling every time I opened my eyes and saw that trophy. First place.

It didn't take long to drift off. When I did, I dreamed Ashley and I were on a ski lift, stuck high over a mountain. The wind whipped our faces and swung the chair so much that Ashley started to freak.

People below waved and told us to hang on, and a shadowy figure raced up the hill. Black hair swung beneath her hat. She pulled a lever and the lift jerked. Ashley screamed and I reached for her, thinking she was going to fall, but I slipped through the chair. The ground came closer, and I saw Lynette smiling.

That's when I woke up. I heard once that you never die in your dreams, and if you do, it's really bad. I looked at my trophy and tried to go back to sleep.

# CHAPTER 7

✖ Ashley ✖

A week and a half later, the finalists were in a meeting with Mr. Gminski, talking about the competition. Bryce and Lynette sat on opposite ends of the first row. Marion sat next to me, chewing on her fingernails.

Mr. Gminski told us what kind of clothes we'd need, that we should bring any special pillows or medicine (I have a seizure disorder), and what the rooms and food would be like. "This is not a plush hotel; it's a dormitory. You'll get a feel for college life."

"How will we get there?" Kael said.

"Mrs. Jarvis is the chaperone for the girls, and she's letting us use her SUV. We'll drive up Wednesday evening and return Sunday."

"Competition Thursday, Friday, and Saturday?" Bryce said.

"Right—they're staggering a few of the events so you'll be able to watch some of the competition," Mr. Gminski said.

He told us about the town and the shops, and I saw Marion cringe. When he finished with the practical stuff, he started the pep talk. "I don't like to compare students, but this is my best team." (One of his former students said he says this every year.) "The addition of Lynette has been wonderful, and all of you worked really hard. I don't think there's another school in the district sending five students."

We all clapped. I wished Hayley were going.

"Practice at least once a day," Mr. Gminski continued. "You'll have to nail each performance perfectly if you want to move on, but I know you all have the ability to do that."

We clapped again. It was the closest I'd ever come to a locker-room speech by a football coach. Forensics is a sport of the mind—remembering stuff, speaking—but it's every bit as nerve-racking as football or basketball. At least that's what I think.

"There's just one more item," Mr. Gminski said, looking at his clipboard. "Payment is due, so I'll need a check no later than tomorrow. Some of you have already paid."

Everyone left but Marion. We'd tried to raise money for her, but all our plans fell through. I stopped at the door and watched Mr. Gminski erase the blackboard. When he turned around, Marion said something.

"Excuse me? I didn't hear that."

"I said I can't go."

"That's preposterous. Of course you can go. You're the best in Impromptu I've ever coached. You may feel a little nervous, but—"

"It's not my nerves. It's the money."

He put the eraser down. "Marion, you're going and that's final."

"I talked with Mom, and she said we can't—"

"Marion," he interrupted, "you're not listening."

"No, *you're* not listening," she said, not in a mean way but in a way that would make you cry if you heard the pain in her voice. "Mom's having money trouble. We can't afford it."

Mr. Gminski smiled at her, and I wanted to kick him. It almost looked like he was making fun of her. He took off his reading glasses and leaned close, like a father checking out a skinned knee. "Marion, don't worry about the money. Someone has agreed to pay your way."

"What?" Marion's mouth dropped. "Who would do that for me?"

"Someone who wanted to remain anonymous," he said. "They believe in you and think you're going to the finals. How you'll pay for that is another matter, but as for RMIFT, you don't have to worry."

Marion covered her face. "Are you serious?"

Mr. Gminski put a hand on her shoulder. "Knock 'em dead up there, kiddo."

PART 2

# CHAPTER 8

◎ *Bryce* ◎

*People think guys don't have feelings,* but it was hard for me to say good-bye to Mom and Sam, even if it was just for a few days. We gathered our suitcases and sleeping bags in front of the school and stowed our stuff in the Jarvises' SUV.

Mom hugged us, which was kind of sappy, but Sam tousled my hair and told me to break a leg. "Not on the ski slope." He winked. Sam's got a good sense of humor for an old guy.

Dylan wouldn't let go of Ashley's neck, and when Mom finally pried him loose, he cried like we were going away forever. Did he know something we didn't? I hadn't told anyone about my dream on the ski lift, but it kind of made me nervous.

Mom hugged Marion. Then Dylan got in on the act, and we had to pry him away from her too. She acted like he was a pest, but I think she really liked the attention. Ashley and I had asked around but couldn't find out who had paid Marion's way.

I got in and waved at everyone. Mr. Gminski drove because he knew the way, and Mrs. Jarvis sat in the front passenger seat. She had chewed me out earlier in the year for an argument I'd had with Lynette, so I tried not to make eye contact with her.

"Are we all ready?" she chirped, as if we were going to a cheerleading competition.

"Rah," Marion said, and I almost laughed out loud.

# CHAPTER 9

Ashley

The drive toward the mountains gave me a chance to think over the past few months. At Christmas, we'd had a surprise guest—Selena Willoby. Bryce and I had returned some money to her during one of our mysteries. She had a good job in Colorado Springs and seemed happy. She gave Bryce an expensive video game and brought me a couple of new candles.

We'd had a string of mysteries over Christmas break, but they'd all fizzled. The most excitement was when Mrs. Watson's dog, Peanuts, ran away and got his head stuck in an empty can of pork and beans. Bryce and I found him in the alley behind Johnny's Pawn and Deli, and it took us a half hour to catch him. We felt bad for him until we got the can off and he nearly bit us. Seemed he liked being in there.

Spiritually, the big news concerned Dylan. Mom had put him to bed one night, but he kept wandering around. I asked what was wrong, and he said, "I'm tired of sleeping."

I put him back in bed and was about to leave when he asked questions about Jesus coming into his heart and forgiving him. I explained the whole thing, not knowing if he would understand, and then he asked if he could pray.

"Sure, buddy," I said. "You can pray right now."

He repeated everything I said with his eyes scrunched tight and his fingers interlaced. The night-light near his bed cast an angelic glow on his face. After he was done, he opened his eyes and said, "Is that it?"

I nodded, even though I know that being a Christian is not just saying a prayer and leaving it at that. But I know God understands the prayers of little kids as well as big ones.

I was about to tell Mom when Dylan called and wanted to know if he could ask Mask Man, his favorite action hero, into his heart so Jesus would have company.

Mom just about lost it when I told her that. I'm still not sure that Dylan gets the whole picture, but God knows his little heart.

As the sun set over the mountain range and my ears popped from the altitude, I thought about the worst part of the past few weeks: Duncan Swift. Our school has a stupid Valentine dance every year. A lot of girls make a big deal about it, and to be honest, I wanted Duncan to ask me.

I had been going through the lunch line behind him as he and some other guys talked about the dance. There were the usual crude comments about girls with braces or who were too fat or skinny.

"Why don't you ask Ashley?" Chuck Burly said, winking at me.

Duncan didn't know I was standing there, and he said, "She's too goofy to take to a dance."

The other guys laughed, but Chuck turned red and looked really sorry.

I ran to my locker and skipped lunch. It was the most awful day of eighth grade. The most awful day of my goofy life.

I had my speech all planned for when Duncan apologized—Chuck surely told him that I had heard him. I'm good at memorizing stuff, so I had a three-point outline of what a friend says and doesn't say about other people. I was going to point out his big nose and ears.

But Duncan never apologized. And he asked Tracy Elliot to the dance.

# CHAPTER 10

☺ *Bryce* ☺

*We parked in front* of a newer building named Harris Hall. Snow was piled high on the sidewalk. Kael and I pulled out the suitcases and stuff from the SUV while Mr. Gminski and Lynette's mom went in to register.

Tres Peaks is a series of three mountains, with pine trees cut like a Mohawk haircut to make room for the ski slopes. We were next to the easternmost peak, which was the tallest and had the most wilderness. We'd passed through the old-fashioned, deserted town. I guessed most students were gone.

The dorm reception area was warm and inviting, and Mr. Gminski had us sign our names and get our room keys. Kael and I were with Mr. Gminski. Marion and Ashley would be with Lynette and her mom.

A guy with long hair and weird eyes moved behind the desk. He wouldn't make eye contact—he just kept looking at the phone and the computer. A stick-on name badge said *Hello, my name is Wendell.* "You guys are the first to arrive," Wendell said. His voice sounded like a walrus gargling. "The others are supposed to get here tomorrow." He pushed photocopied diagrams of the campus toward us and explained the layout of the college. "You're right here. The elevator is here. Our rooms are set up in suites. You'll each have your own bedroom that's connected to a living area and a bathroom. You can use your sleeping bags, or if you need linens, they're in housekeeping down the hall."

"Do we have to be careful and not touch stuff in the rooms?" Marion said.

"You'll see books on the shelves and some personal items," Wendell said, "but the students cleared out most of their stuff. You can use the computers in the dining area to check e-mail if you want."

Mr. Gminski turned to us. "Find your rooms, get settled, and meet down here in 20 minutes."

# CHAPTER 11

�֍ Ashley �֍

I was excited to see our suite. We rode the elevator and got off on the fifth floor—the guys were on the sixth. The hallways smelled like they'd been freshly painted, and the carpet was clean. I've seen dorm rooms in movies and once visited a friend at Colorado Christian University, so I figured things would be pretty cramped, but I was blown away by our room.

"I think I know where I want to go to college," Lynette said, looking at the couch, TV, and kitchenette.

My thoughts exactly.

The bedrooms were small, each with a bed, a desk, and a built-in closet and dresser, but they felt cozy. Unlike the others, my bed still had clothes and shoes on and around it, which seemed weird, plus the desk was piled high with books and papers.

Someone knocked on the outer door, and a pretty brown-haired girl with bright eyes and a beautiful smile welcomed us. She was in great shape, with muscular arms and legs. She held a scroll of paper and waved it around as she talked.

"I'm Jennifer Zeal—you can call me Jen. I'm the RA assigned to the floor, so if you need anything, just ask. I'll be here through the weekend in the room next to the elevator."

I waved to her. "My room has stuff in it. Should I just move it, or . . . ? "

Jen came inside, peeked in my room, and shook her head. "This is Vanessa's room. She was supposed to have it cleared out. I'll get you a box."

"She looks like a movie star," Marion whispered when Jen left.

"She looks like a wrestler," Lynette said.

Jen came back, and I carefully put Vanessa's clothes and shoes in the box. I didn't bother with the desk—I figured I could do that later.

We walked to the elevator and passed a wall covered with posters and announcements—used cars for sale, apartments for rent, people needing rides, and a big poster about an audition for a film. It gave the director's name and said his company was casting a female—late teens, early 20s—"for a serious film about love and loss in the college years." It gave the time of the Thursday audition, where to pick up a script, and how to register.

Jen's door was open, and I heard her on the phone asking about Vanessa. "Really?" she said. "Well, she's not here, and she didn't clean out her room. I thought maybe she'd gone home, but with the audition tomorrow . . . No, I didn't see her at play practice either. . . ." Jen saw us and waved.

I noticed the rolled-up paper on a chair and guessed it was a script.

# CHAPTER 12

☺ *Bryce* ☺

*Mr. Gminski walks fast,* especially when it's cold. We could see our breath floating like ghosts along the sidewalk. We passed real-estate offices advertising mountain properties, chalets, and cabins. The restaurant was only a few blocks away, but it was so cold that I thought my teeth were going to chatter out of my head.

A man in a long coat met us. He shook Mr. Gminski's hand and told us he was Professor Hopper.

"The professor is the one who got us in early," Mr. Gminski said.

The restaurant was called Top Billing, and the walls were covered with film posters and pictures of stars, some with autographs. There were also stills from movies, old and new, and stenciled on the walls were famous quotations from movies. Wooden benches lined the walls, and there were two pool tables in the back. It looked like a college-student paradise.

A cute waitress with curly brown hair took our orders.

Everyone got hot chocolate and looked at the menu. I wasn't going to get anything until Mr. Gminski said he was paying. I ordered a basket of onion rings.

The waitress smiled. "Great choice—it's the best thing on the menu."

"Some pretty famous people have gone to school at CSD," Mr. Hopper said as we waited for our food. He rattled off some names, and I recognized most of them. "There's a tour of the campus in the morning—if you're interested."

Ashley's eyes sparkled. College seemed like a million years away to me, but she loves to plan.

The food arrived, and Mr. Gminski dug into a hamburger the size of a small cow and wiped his face with a napkin.

Ashley asked about some audition for a movie part, and Professor Hopper said it was closed. No one could watch.

Kael helped me eat the onion rings, and then it was time for dessert. I ordered their Pitt of Chocolate—named after Brad—a big chocolate shell with chocolate ice cream and Hershey's Kisses on top, smothered in chocolate syrup. I was halfway through when I had to stop. I figured I would bleed black if someone stuck me with a pin.

It felt even colder walking back to the dorm, and a light snow began. Mr. Gminski talked with the professor the whole way. I noticed lights near the bottom of the ski slopes and couldn't wait to get there. I hoped they wouldn't keep us cooped up doing tours the whole day.

"Weather's supposed to turn nasty tomorrow," Marion said.

"Great!" Kael said.

"Ditto," I said.

**CHAPTER 13**

❀ Ashley ❀

A campus-security vehicle was parked in front of the dorm. I didn't think much about it until we got off the elevator and saw two guys in uniforms in our room.

"Sorry to bother you, ladies," a guy said. "I'm just checking out Vanessa's room."

"What's wrong?" Mrs. Jarvis said.

"Probably nothing. We're doing a search of the building."

Jen came out of her room, looking shaken. "I'm sorry. I'm just worried. Vanessa has a part-time job off campus, and she didn't show up today. Her mother hasn't heard from her, and she doesn't answer her cell phone."

I'd heard enough stories about missing college students, especially females, to raise my caution meter. It seemed like every day you heard about someone who left work and didn't come home. I looked at Marion, and I could tell she was deep in thought.

"She's supposed to audition tomorrow, right?" I said to Jen.

"Yeah. And she's really good. One of the best in the school."

We waited until the security guys finished, then entered the room. They had put everything on Vanessa's desk into another cardboard box and shoved it into the closet.

Lynette and her mom wanted to watch a movie, and Marion joined them, but I was tired. I stayed in my room with the door closed, staring at the box.

My mind spun with scary ideas, and I grabbed the phone and dialed Bryce's room. There was a hockey game on in the background when he picked up. I told him about Vanessa, that I was in her room, and that security guys were searching for her.

"They're on our floor right now," Bryce said, "but there's nobody else up here."

"Don't you have an RA?"

"A what?"

"Resident advisor." I told him about Jen.

"I'll check," Bryce said. "Let me know if you hear anything."

I hung up and looked at the box. I couldn't help myself. I went to the closet and dumped everything onto the floor.

# CHAPTER 14

☺ *Bryce* ☺

*As soon as the security guys left,* I looked for the RA and noticed snow leading from the elevator to the door. Had the security guys tracked it in?

I knocked on the RA's door and waited. I heard Kael whoop and cheer, and I felt bad that I had missed an Avalanche goal. I was about to leave when a curly-haired guy opened the door. He looked like he'd just stepped out of an REI catalog. He was wearing a North Face sweater, goggles, and gloves. Snow pants were hanging on a peg on the wall, and wet boots sat by the door.

"You guys are here early, huh?" he said with a smile and extending a hand. "I'm Hunter Roth. You're with the forensics tournament, right?"

I told him my name and shook his hand.

"Avs fan?"

I nodded. "My sister said something about a missing girl—Vanessa . . ."

"Vanessa Harvey? She's one of the best actresses in school. What makes you think she's missing?"

I told him what we'd heard, and he scratched his stubbly chin. I wondered if I'd ever get that rugged, outdoorsy, hair-on-the-chin look that seemed to come naturally to guys like Hunter.

"Let me call my girlfriend and find out what she knows. Thanks for the tip."

I went back to my room and tried to concentrate on the Avs game, but I couldn't.

I walked to the side window and stared at the falling snow. It looked like some postcard photo you send to people to make them jealous of your vacation.

Already I felt the connection with Ashley. We were on the hunt again, being drawn into something bigger than both of us. Vanessa was in trouble.

*Maybe she's out with her boyfriend tonight or at a movie with friends. Or maybe she's really excited about the audition and just needed to get away. Or she's afraid she'll fail and wind up waiting tables at Top Billing for the rest of her life.*

*Or maybe some madman kidnapped her.*

# CHAPTER 15

❀ Ashley ❀

I stared at a college student's life on the closet floor. If Vanessa was as confused about her life as I was, she was in deep trouble. I found a box of diet pills right next to several candy bars. Books were piled on top of the stack—everything from literature to advanced math. Her assignment notebooks were filled with notes. She had flawless handwriting, but the ideas meandered like a lazy river. I could read them, but I couldn't make much sense of them. I also found some nicotine gum, which made me think she'd been trying to stop smoking.

Her clothes had tags from well-known designers and looked expensive, except for some ratty shorts and hole-filled socks. Toward the bottom of the pile was a year-old calendar. Class schedules and times filled the boxes. Some weeks had lines through them and said *play practice,* while one week in the summer said *vacation.* She also listed her work times along with names and phone numbers.

I looked for any notes that said *met my dream man today* or something like that, but I didn't find any.

"You okay?" someone said, and I jumped. It was Marion wearing a Save the Whales nightgown with a big whale flipping on the front. She sat cross-legged on the floor.

"Just going through some of Vanessa's stuff," I said. "I'm getting worried."

"Ashley Timberline on an investigation." Marion smirked. "I get to watch the master."

I wanted to slug her whale in the blowhole. "Stop. I've just got a bad feeling."

"Snow's really coming down outside," Marion said. "Hope she didn't drive her car off the side of some slick road."

"Wait. Does she have a car?"

Marion shook her head. "How should I know?"

I picked up the phone and dialed Jen's room. "Does Vanessa have a car of her own?"

"Yeah, an old beater." She gave me a description.

When I hung up, Marion was staring at a leather-bound book, a weird look on her face. "I think you should see this."

It was a diary of sorts. Vanessa had written bits of dialogue from movies and novels and her reactions. In the corner she recorded the date.

October 17
    Final preparations for Romeo and Juliet. Bummed that I didn't get a lead. Jen Zeal is understudying me, and I'm not impressed. She can act, but behind the scenes, I get the feeling she's out to get me.

# CHAPTER 16

☺ *Bryce* ☺

*I wanted to crawl into my sleeping bag* after the Avs game because I was exhausted, but Ashley's words sent my mystery antennae up. I snuck down the back stairs, and the door closed, echoing through the stairwell. There's something about being alone in a strange place that makes everything spooky.

I made it to the first floor and stopped at the back door. Ashley had described the parking lot as only a short distance from our building. I had forgotten my key card, so I found a pebble, wedged it in the doorjamb, and let the door close, testing it before I went outside.

The other thing I'd forgotten was my coat. The snow was really coming down. I crossed the parking lot but didn't see a second lot behind it. I climbed up a snowbank, keeping my hands in my pockets.

Then I saw it. About a football field away was another lot with a few cars, all covered with snow.

I took off in a dead run to keep the blood flowing and was out of breath when I arrived. We live at about 7,000 feet, but Tres Peaks is at least 11,000 feet so there's less oxygen.

Ashley didn't have the license-plate number, but she had a good description. I located Vanessa's rusted car with a dent in the driver's-side door. The windows were covered with snow, so I cleared some off using my elbow. (I've lived in cold places long enough not to use my bare hand.)

Nothing in the front seat but some books and a purse.

*Why would a girl go off and leave her purse?* I thought.

I scraped at the back window. Ice was caked underneath, and I had to move around to get a good look.

I gasped.

A face, looking back. White as a sheet. Lifeless.

I stumbled and fell, both hands plunging into the snow. My heart beat like crazy.

I ran for the dorm, which now seemed a million miles away. Each step left me panting. Finally I reached the back door and pulled.

Locked.

The pebble wasn't there.

I banged on the door, peering through a small window. Nothing moved inside. I banged again.

Someone jumped in front of the door. It was Kael. "What are you doing out there, Timberline?"

"Did you move that rock?"

"Yeah, I followed you down here and thought I'd scare you. But it looks like somebody beat me to it."

"Find a phone."

**CHAPTER 17**

❀ Ashley ❀

The security guys came after Bryce and I called, and we headed for the parking lot. They let Bryce and me ride with them. I thought back on all the mysteries we'd helped solve. There were plenty of times when we thought we might find a dead body, but it had never happened. The thought of Vanessa, whose diary I had just read, freezing in the back of her car made me sick. Why would she do it? Or had someone put her there?

Bryce pointed the way, and the driver turned into the snow-filled lot. He turned on a bright light and read the license-plate number.

"That's her car," the other guard said.

Bryce opened his door.

"We want you to stay here," the driver said.

The guards left the car running, the heater on high.

"Should we tell Mr. Gminski?" I said, my teeth chattering.

Bryce didn't answer. He seemed in another world, staring through the frosty windshield. "I wonder what happened. If Vanessa did it on purpose, or if she went to sleep inside and the temperature dropped. . . ."

The security guys tried to open the car, but the doors were either locked or frozen. Steam swirled from their mouths like clouds. The driver returned and grabbed a scraper from the front seat, then hacked at the ice on Vanessa's car like a lumberjack.

The driver clicked on his flashlight and pointed it into the backseat. The beam of light cast an eerie glow through the snow, and I could see the outline of a head.

Police and people who deal with crime get used to seeing bad stuff. They joke about it. But I was not prepared to see the security guys laugh. They pointed at the backseat and bent over, and one banged his knee with a hand.

Bryce flew out of the car, and I followed.

The two men were hooting now, shaking their heads.

"Is it her?" Bryce said.

# CHAPTER 18

☺ *Bryce* ☺

*"A mannequin?"* Kael said, trying not to laugh.

The security guards had dropped Ashley and me at Harris Hall and driven away, still laughing.

"It looked real with all that snow and ice," I said.

"Did it have hair?" Marion said. She wasn't laughing, but by the way her upper lip twitched, I figured it wouldn't be long.

I shook my head.

"That's pretty good, Timberline. The case of the frozen dummy." Kael punched my arm. "Plus, you found that bald mannequin."

"Funny," I said.

"Did security say how the mannequin was killed?" Kael added.

"At least that explains where Vanessa got all those nice clothes," Ashley said. I could tell she was trying to put a good spin on this.

"What do you mean?" Marion said.

"The security guys said she works at a dress shop called Melanie's," Ashley said. "They sell high-end stuff."

"But why would she have a dummy in the backseat?" Marion said.

"I hear those dummies are all over," Kael said, pushing my shoulder.

"Some girls who work late put those in their cars to make people think they're not alone," Ashley said.

"Is that a problem around here?" Marion said.

"You bet," someone said behind us. It was Wendell, the night guy. "Last semester a group of girls went to a late show. One girl forgot her purse and went back inside. When she came out, her friends had left, but somebody followed her home.

"The next week, another woman reported the same thing, only this time she saw his face and described him to the police."

"They ever catch him?" Marion said.

"You can't put a guy in jail for driving behind someone." He grinned. "But around Thanksgiving they found an abandoned car in a ravine that matched the description both women had given."

"Nobody inside?" I said.

"Nope. Nothing but a bloody knife."

"How awful," Ashley said.

"That sounds like a bad movie plot," Kael said, squinting.

Wendell held up a stack of stapled pages. "Got a B+ in Screen-writing for it."

## CHAPTER 19

❀ Ashley ❀

My alarm rang early the next morning. I hadn't slept well, and the bed was a lot harder than it looked. Lynette and her mom had already gone to breakfast (nice of them to wait), but Marion was in the living room watching an early news show.

"Snow's stopped for now, but there's supposed to be a big blast headed our way," Marion said. "Wouldn't it be something if we got snowed in? All those cute forensics types hanging around?"

"You mean like my brother?" I said.

"I wasn't mentioning any names, but . . ." She muted the sound. "Ashley, tell me the truth. Do you think I have a chance?"

"To be friends?" I said. "A great chance. I just don't think Bryce is that interested in—"

"He's interested in Lynette. You'd have to be from another planet not to notice that."

"But Lynette hates his guts. She's made his life miserable the past few months."

"Exactly. Maybe if I tried the same thing he'd get interested in me. You know—tear down a monument to his friend, trash his faith in class, embarrass him in front of the school. Why do guys always go for the girls who hurt them?"

I wanted to tell Marion in a kind way that she had about as much chance of being Bryce's girlfriend as I had of being Duncan's, but I didn't have the heart. Besides, a commotion outside took us into the hall as kids arrived with their gear. Girls ran from the elevator, laughing, throwing sleeping bags and pillows at each other.

Jen was in crisis mode, scratching her head with a pencil and trying to answer questions. I wanted to just go to breakfast, but she looked like she could use some help.

"Would you?" she said when I offered. "That would be great. Just help the girls at the end of the hall find the linen room downstairs."

I recognized one girl from a competition earlier in the year. Then another girl who competes in my event—with perfect hair, perfect diction, and killer material. Was she standing between me and a trip to California?

**CHAPTER 20**

◑ *Bryce* ◐

*The dining hall served a limited breakfast*—juice, do-nuts, cereal, and frozen waffles. I didn't mind because I wasn't really hungry. I was still licking my wounds over the dummy in the car. A security guard passed and smirked, munching a donut. Maybe it was just me, but it felt like everyone was looking and grinning.

I wanted to sit with Kael, but Lynette was with him. Instead, I found the desk worker, Wendell, looking at the morning paper and tossing down bear claws like they were on the endangered pastries list.

"Can I sit here?" I said.

"Sure, Sherlock," he said without looking up. Leigh calls me the same thing, and it drives me crazy. "You know, even though it turned out bad, it was smart to check her car. Those security guys hadn't thought of it."

"There's nothing in there about Vanessa, is there?"

He shook his head. "Avs won, though."

"Yeah, I saw most of it."

"My guess is, she'll be back by noon."

"Really? How do you figure that?"

He turned the paper around and showed me a picture of Peter Valance, the famous actor and director. I'd seen him in a couple of Mom's old movies. The headline read "Acclaimed Director Looking for Tres Peaks Talent."

"He's coming today," Wendell said. "And Vanessa is about the best. She'll show up."

"About the best? Is there someone better?"

"A few who might fit his script better. You know, taller, thinner, fatter—whatever."

"You should show him your script about the killer who follows girls home," I said.

He closed the paper and tapped a stack of pages about two inches thick. "Got something else in mind for him."

For some reason, I'm able to read stuff upside down. The title of the script was *Scream Test*. I figured it was another one of those teenage slasher movies I'd heard about. "Can I see it?"

He pursed his lips, then shoved the pages toward me.

I flipped through them.

*MELINDA*
*(scared) I don't think we should be in here.*

BART
*(making fun of her) Chicken.*
*(makes chicken noises) You can't let an old house freak you out.*


MELINDA
*You heard what that old lady down the road said. It's haunted.*


BART
*Look, we'll stay here overnight. Tomorrow you'll meet with that*
*producer guy, and you'll be on your way to Hollywood.*
*(Eerie noises in background.)*


Wendell grabbed the script from me before I could read any more.

"Looks good," I said. "You're really going to show it to him?"

"If those girls don't take up all his time," Wendell said, his teeth clenched. "Actors get the attention and glory. Nobody wants to hear what writers say at the Academy Awards. They only want to hear the people with pretty faces."

I was about to ask another question when I sensed someone behind me. I turned and saw Mr. Gminski.

"I need to see you and your sister. Now."

**CHAPTER 21**

❦ Ashley ❦

I helped some girls find their linens, then found Jen with another group. Breakfast was almost over, and Marion and I had to hustle just to get cereal before the milk ran out. In the middle of some Corn Flakes, Bryce and Mr. Gminski appeared.

"Marion, would you mind giving us a moment?" Mr. Gminski said.

As Marion walked away, she looked at Bryce and me like we were about to walk the plank.

Mr. Gminski raked some cereal dust into a neat pile. After a couple of minutes, which seemed like a couple of hours, he spoke. "You are two of my best students. My most trusted students. I can always

depend on you to be leaders when it comes to behavior and following rules."

"We didn't—," Bryce tried to say.

Mr. Gminski held up a hand. "The head of security said you were
snooping around a parking lot. Leaving the building after dark is for-
bidden. You knew that, didn't you?"

Bryce just looked at the cereal pile and nodded.

I wanted to tell Mr. Gminski that it had been my idea, but I kept
my mouth shut.

"I didn't expect this out of you." Mr. Gminski talked like we were
bad little puppies. We were trying to help find a lost girl, but I could
see his point. "I have every right to call your parents and have them
take you home."

The old call-your-parents threat was a good one, since neither
Bryce nor I wanted to leave.

Mom taught me a long time ago that when people act angry it can
mean a lot of different things. It could be that they've gotten a speed-
ing ticket that day or their cat got run over by a car or their teenager
is in trouble. Maybe Mr. Gminski was worried about what Mr. Book-
man, our principal, would say.

"We're really sorry," I said. "I found out about the missing girl—
I'm staying in her room—and my mind started going and I thought
we could actually help her."

His eyes softened. I think he'd expected us to snap at him.

"It won't happen again," Bryce said. "Even if I'm thirsty and want to
get a drink at the water fountain, I'll make sure I check out with you."

He rolled his eyes. "I don't want to come down hard on you, but a
lot is at stake here."

I wondered what he meant, but I didn't ask. I just watched him
get up and leave.

# CHAPTER 22

☺ *Bryce* ☺

*I didn't want to take the tour of the campus,* but I knew that Mr. Gminski wouldn't like it if I slipped off to the ski slopes. I needed to clear my head, but I followed like a lemming anyway.

We broke into a few different groups. Our tour guide, Lynda, (she made a big deal about being Lynda with a *y*) didn't look much older than Leigh, who's a senior in high school. Lynda was shorter than Ashley and had a higher-pitched voice than a Saturday-morning-cartoon character.

"This is Smith Hall, where most of our English courses are taught,"

Lynda said. "Literature classes and all different types of writing—novels, poetry, screenwriting, and journalism."

"So everybody is segmented?" Marion said. "Film and TV on one side of the campus and writers on the other?"

"Everyone takes the same core classes, but there are different creative disciplines. Video people tend to hang with each other, directors stick together, and actors break off and do their own thing. It's normal."

We walked toward a round brick building with lots of windows circling the top. People's faces were carved into a cement section that ran around the middle, and I recognized a couple of writers' faces. It was the coolest library I'd ever seen.

I like to read sports biographies and mysteries, but just about every shelf had something interesting. The building was almost empty, so Lynda squealed in her normal voice. A light was on in one side room, and I backed away from our group to get a look. What I saw made my jaw drop. It was the RA from our floor, Hunter, with a girl who looked strong enough to wrestle him to the ground. They were in a heated discussion.

Ashley joined me. "Who's Jen talking to?"

"You know that girl?" I said.

"Our RA."

"Would you mind rejoining us up here?" Lynda said.

We did, but I wished I had a recorder to stick inside that room.

# CHAPTER 23

Ashley

As we took the tour, everyone sized up the competition. We finally made it to the auditorium. As it turned out, there were several on campus, but the biggest was in a building by itself. They held plays, concerts, and anything that needed seats for more than a few hundred people. Even some stand-up comedians had been there.

Lynda led us inside the cavernous building. The doors slammed with a monstrous echo. I imagined the place full of people, clapping for someone onstage. Empty, it just looked lonely.

She talked about all the plays performed here—everything from Shakespeare to ones written by students. A poster advertised the current production, and I pointed out Vanessa's picture to Bryce.

Lynda looked at her watch. "In another hour a graduate of the school will conduct an audition for an upcoming movie, and we're hoping one of our own students will be in the production."

We walked through the music building, another massive structure, and strolled through exhibits of weird drawings and sculptures in the art building.

Lynda took us by a huge cafeteria that was closed—we'd been eating in one of the dorm dining halls—then finished by taking us outside and up to a little knoll overlooking the school. "One of the perks of going to CSD is the natural beauty. Our ski lift is open—it should get even better if the weather forecast is right—and just up the road is the Rocky Mountain National Park. Parents visit their kids here and wind up staying."

One kid pointed at a grove of aspens as something moved into a clearing.

"That's Phil, our honorary elk," Lynda said. "He'll wander around campus looking for food." She gestured at the science building and a smooth area on the rough bricks. "He loves to rub his horns right at that spot, and it makes a scary sound. But don't try to pet him; he's wild."

"Are there different slopes for advanced and beginners?" Bryce asked.

"Sure. Everyone takes the rope to the top. You can take the bunny trail or the steeper one. There's also a cross-country route."

The rope was on a pulley system, with tires at the top and bottom spinning the rope. People grabbed it and were whisked away. It was kind of low budget compared with all the upscale resorts around, but it got the job done.

Someone asked about skis and snowboards, and Lynda motioned to a small building. I could tell Bryce couldn't wait.

# CHAPTER 24

☺ *Bryce* ☺

*My first round* was scheduled for early afternoon, so I went to get my script. Even though I have the thing memorized, you have to hold it during the routine. Mom had laminated it, and I'd added a ring to flip the pages easier.

I called her on my cell phone, and she sounded sad, like she wished she could be here. Dylan was home from kindergarten with a cough, so I talked with him. He wanted me to play hockey. I wear Rollerblades and smack a tennis ball into our net. He tries to block my shots and squeals when he does.

When I finished, I turned the phone off and put it in my jacket

pocket. I decided not to eat because I have lots of movement in my
routine. You have to keep one foot planted, like a pivot foot in basketball, but you can move around a lot. I knew I had to perform the
piece after seeing a high schooler do it. I try to put my special
touches on the different voices.

I got to the room early and put my jacket on a chair. People were
already getting good seats. One judge wrote our order on the blackboard. (I was fourth out of six.) A judge said we'd begin in five minutes, and I hurried to the bathroom.

Another contestant was there trying to get his hair to lie down.
He waved and smiled. "You're the guy who does 'Good Morning,'
right?"

I nodded. "And you do the routine about the hunter." I had to
smile. The thing was really funny, in a deadpan kind of way. "Hope
you do well."

"Yeah, you too."

I walked back to the room and passed Kael. "Break a leg, Timberline," he said.

"Thanks."

Marion Quidley had taken a seat in the front row when I got
there. She was all smiles.

*Great,* I thought.

**CHAPTER 25**

❀ Ashley ❀

My first round wasn't until 4 p.m., so I went back to the auditorium to get a look at the director and the students going into the audition. To my surprise, one of the doors was open. As I went inside to stay warm, I imagined muscular security guards handcuffing me, but I had to see the place again. I moseyed up the stairs to the balcony.

I expected to see a bunch of cameras and a big set, but the lights lit a bare stage.

I said a prayer for Bryce because his competition was about to begin. I had just said, "Amen" when the door opened and a bunch of people arrived. My heart raced and I froze, thinking I was in big trouble. Instead of heading for the door, I hunkered down by the railing.

*Why do I get into these situations?*

A woman with frizzy hair led a group of more than a dozen young women to stage right, then behind a curtain. As she gave directions, a guy set up a small camera on a platform, and a man in a leather jacket sauntered toward the front. Frizzy Hair came out and handed him some pages, and the man put on small glasses.

The first student shielded her eyes from the lights. She stood on an *X* made with duct tape and faced the camera.

"Just tell us your name and where you're from and maybe something about yourself," the director said. His voice was hoarse, like he had a cold.

"Okay," she said, then giggled. She gave her name and said she was from Kansas.

"Like Dorothy," the director said.

"What? Oh, *The Wizard of Oz*. Right. Dorothy. Click your heels and all that."

There was an awkward pause. Finally the director said, "All right, let's do the scene. I'll throw you the first line. Any questions?"

She shook her head and looked at the page, then dropped it on the stage.

"Olivia, I've watched you these past few months," the director said. "I've seen the way you care. I love you."

The girl from Kansas began, but there was something missing. It was like she was reading the lines off a teleprompter in her head. There was no emotion.

The second girl, from Taos, New Mexico, had way too much emotion. They nearly had to carry her off the stage because of her overacting.

The director paid attention to each person, smiling when she was done and saying, "Thank you."

I kept waiting for Vanessa to walk onstage, but she wasn't in the lineup.

Fourteen girls performed before Jen walked out. She wore a pretty pleated skirt and a sweater that made her look more feminine. I wondered how long she'd stood in front of her closet trying to pick out the right outfit.

"I'm Jennifer Zeal, a senior here at CSD—thank you for what you've done at the school, Mr. Valance."

The director smiled politely.

He threw her the line, and Jen picked up on it perfectly, not too dramatic, playing the character close to the vest. She basically nailed the part, and when she finished, it was all I could do not to stand up and clap.

"Very nice, Jennifer," the director said. "Thank you for coming."

She nodded and walked away.

I wanted to get out so I quietly stood. The seat creaked like an old door hinge in one of those bad horror movies.

Before I could duck, Frizzy Hair looked my way. "You there!" she yelled. "What are you doing?"

# CHAPTER 26

☾ *Bryce* ☾

*The contestants were good,* and the more I tried to shut that thought out, the more nervous I became. Mr. Gminski was right. This was a whole new level of competition.

The guy with the hunting story got up, turned on his best Appalachian accent, and began. "The stars was out, and me and my friend Harlan was deep in the woods. His dawg treed somethin', and I thought it might be a coon, maybe a possum. But when I held that lantern out and saw those beady eyes lookin' down at me, I knew what we'd found. A lynx. Never seen one before. And if we could knock it out and get its hide, we'd both be rich."

The boy dropped his head, then looked up. Using another voice, he explained that the two characters were kids of the Depression, out looking for food when they came upon a lynx whose pelt was worth lots of money.

He used different voices for the two characters, then added a third, a man whose gun the two borrowed. When it came time to shoot the animal, all three fought over it. Finally, the gun owner said he'd do it and pulled the trigger.

The boy studied the floor, spat a fake chaw of tobacco juice, and looked at the audience. "You mean to tell me you dragged me out of bed at two in the morning and all the way down this hill just to shoot my wife's cat?"

It was a great ending, and everybody laughed.

Then came the dull part, where you sit around and wait for the judges to make notes and tabulate the score. At the end they ranked each contestant.

Marion Quidley turned and raised her eyebrows, as if to say, *Pretty stiff competition.* I didn't need Marion's opinion.

Moments dragged. The only thing you could hear was the sound of red pencils on paper.

One judge looked at me and nodded, and I made my way to the front. You have to wait for all three judges to look at you, so I stood there, trying to keep my stomach quiet.

One girl in the corner snickered, and that sent ripples of nervous laughter through the crowd.

I glanced out the back window at the dorm and the hillside beyond. A beautiful scene. I wondered if this was as close as I would come to Hollywood.

The final judge put his pencil down and smiled, interlacing his fingers. It was showtime.

I began my routine with the usual flair, introducing my comedic piece about military life in Iraq and a blogger who wrote daily notes to the troops. It was going well until I was interrupted by a ring.

I looked around the room and tried to keep going, the sweat starting to form on top of my lip. That's when I recognized the sound. A cell phone. The judges had given strict instructions for everyone to turn their phones off.

And the ringtone was unmistakably mine.

# CHAPTER 27

✖ Ashley ✖

My stomach churned, and my heart beat faster as I ducked behind the row of seats. I prayed they would think I was a mouse.

"Excuse me?" Frizzy Hair snapped. "This is a closed audition. What are you doing up there?"

I got ready for the handcuffs, but no security guard came.

"Come on, honey," the director said. "Stand up. We're not going to bite your head off."

I put a hand on the seat and stood. My head felt like it was roasting at 350 degrees.

Frizzy Hair put her hands on her hips. "Young lady—," she began.

Peter Valance held up a hand. "Come on down here."

I looked behind me, then back at him. "Me?"

He smiled. "Yeah, come on." He turned to Frizzy Hair. "How many do we have left?"

"I think there's one more."

I made it to the balcony stairs and considered hitting the Exit door. When I got to the bottom of the stairs, the last girl was onstage, standing at the *X,* giving her name and information.

Frizzy Hair motioned for me to sit.

When the girl finished (she was almost as good as Jen), the director wrote something in a black book, then turned to me. "You want to give it a try?"

"Oh, Peter, please," Frizzy Hair said.

"Come on, Eleanor. If she had enough chutzpah to sneak in here, she might as well try."

To Eleanor's chagrin, I walked toward the stage. My legs felt like Frankenstein's, but I finally made it. "I'm only in the eighth grade," I apologized. "I'm here for the forensics competition and—"

"It's okay," Peter said. "It'll be a good experience. Something you can tell your kids about someday, right?"

"I don't even have a script."

"Eleanor, give her a script."

Eleanor had one left, and she gave it to me like it was the last life preserver on the *Titanic.*

"Stand on the *X* and tell us about yourself."

If I had planned this, I'm sure I would have been even more nervous, but something took over. Maybe it's from my gymnastics competitions or the forensics, or it could be all the crazy stuff Bryce and I do using cameras and making up stupid movies, but a little piece of my brain clicked and I walked on that stage like I knew exactly what I was doing.

I took a deep breath and let it out.

The guy behind the camera nodded and smiled, like I was his kid sister.

"My name is Ashley Timberline. I'm in the eighth grade at Red Rock Middle School—in Red Rock, Colorado. Uh, my mom has some of your movies from a long time ago—she is not going to believe I'm doing this."

"Why did you sneak in here?" Peter said.

"Well, two reasons. One is, I really want to act someday. Movies or plays. And the other is because there's a girl missing. Vanessa. I'm staying in her room, and I hoped she'd show up here."

"Vanessa Harvey," Eleanor said, checking her list. "Didn't show."

The director nodded and looked at me with his deep blue eyes. "All right, you've watched the scene a few times; you should have a feel for it. Olivia is in love with Brian, but Brian is in love with Stephanie. This scene is with Brian's best friend, Tim, who is madly in love with Olivia, though she hasn't given him the time of day."

It was all complicated, but as he repeated the lead-in, I took another breath.

# CHAPTER 28

☺ *Bryce* ☺

*Mr. Gminski has taught us* that once you start your routine, you keep going no matter what. He even put us through a drill by letting his two-year-old son walk around the room while we practiced. We had to keep going and not laugh as the kid sat on a whoopee cushion or blew a noisemaker. It wasn't easy.

But this was different. This was my phone ringing, with a special ringtone that played a favorite song. That song was quickly becoming the worst in history.

As soon as the phone rang, people started looking at each other. The judges just stared at me.

On the third ring, kids laughed or held hands over their mouths and tried not to laugh, which made it worse. It was like thinking of something funny in church and not being able to laugh—it just makes you laugh more. Something mildly funny can become nuclear funny when you're supposed to be quiet.

The middle judge held up a hand. "Will whoever has the cell phone please turn it off?"

"Sir, it's mine," I said. "I thought I turned it off earlier."

He motioned to my seat, and I hurried to my jacket. If this was Ashley calling, I'd kill her later, but the screen said *Unavailable.*

"I'm really sorry," I said as I took my place.

The judges spoke to each other quietly.

"Mr. Timberline," the middle judge finally said, "the rules give us latitude to allow you to start over or pick up where you were." He tapped his pencil lightly. "My colleagues have decided to give mercy. You can start again."

I felt like I could reach down my throat and touch my heart—it was that close. I nodded to the other two judges, obviously fine people who knew what it was like to make a mistake.

"I hope you'll learn from this, Mr. Timberline," the middle judge said. "Begin."

# CHAPTER 29

❀ Ashley ❀

"Maybe she should do her forensics routine," Eleanor said when I took too long to start.

The director stared at me. "This scene is supposed to be emotional, like what you're saying is tearing your heart out. Ever have something like that happen?"

I nodded. "My dad died a few years ago . . . in a plane crash."

The room fell deathly silent, and he looked at his script. "I'm sorry. Maybe you don't want to—"

"No, please," I said. "I want to try."

The director held out a hand. "The stage is yours, Ashley."

I checked the script, but I was really remembering the day I'd found out about Dad. It didn't seem real until the news flashed pictures of the plane washing ashore. That's when it became real. Dad wasn't coming back.

I could feel the emotion when I began. "Tim, I really like you. You're funny. You care about people. I'm flattered you would care about me, but I can't dredge up feelings that aren't there." I bit my lip and felt tears. "I don't want to hurt you. I wish none of this would have happened, and I'd give anything if I could feel the same. But I don't."

The script went on, but I had hit the emotional high (or low) and my chin quivered.

The director raised his eyebrows. "You're good."

I shot a glance at Eleanor, who stood with her mouth open.

"Eleanor, have her sign a release with her address and phone number," he said.

"At her age, we need her parents' consent. . . ."

He fumbled with papers, gathering his things. "Well, we know this part's not right for her, but there might be something in the future. Just a formality." He looked at me. "Keep practicing—you're going somewhere with that talent."

I tried to say something, but when I opened my mouth, nothing came out.

Eleanor brought me a piece of paper, and my hands shook as I wrote down my information. "Do you know how many people would kill for a chance at what you just did?" she said.

The camera guy said, "Good job."

"What about the others?" I said to Eleanor. "Will any of them get a part?"

Eleanor frowned. "To be honest, I was hoping for more talent.

There were a couple of girls who were close." She rolled her eyes as the director walked out with a cell phone to his ear. "Who knows how he'll feel one day to the next. Jennifer was good, but she's a little too buff for the part." She paused. "That story about your father. Is it true?"

I nodded, then told her about the whole thing. She listened as she packed up her own stuff. When I told her my mom had met Sam at one of the memorial services, she looked away.

"What?" I said.

"I'm always thinking about stories. Your mother's sounds interesting. And you say she's a writer?" She pulled out a card with her name on it. "Tell your mom to drop me an e-mail. I'd like to talk with her."

**CHAPTER 30**

☺ *Bryce* ☺

*The audience clapped,* but I felt like I'd just been through the 10 most grueling minutes of my life. I'd tried to snap out of the phone fiasco, but a cloud hung over my performance. I distinctly remembered turning my phone off after talking to Mom.

Marion caught my eye and gave me a thumbs-up. She had to know I'd just laid an egg.

The last two contestants were okay, but they had some mechanical problems. Staying in character. Too much or too little movement. I had no idea where I'd place and just wanted to get out of the room.

"You did great considering the phone," Marion said as she caught up. "Aren't you going to stick around and see your score?"

"I'll be lucky to get third," I said. "I'm going back to the dorm."

"Okay, I'll stay and find out for you."

I took the long walk across campus, eyeing the clouds. The Colorado sunshine is legendary, but today was overcast, like the hovering clouds had hidden the sun in a back drawer.

I found Ashley at a telephone in Harris Hall, beaming. She hadn't competed, so why was she so excited?

"Bryce is here," she said, then covered the phone. "It's Mom. How did you do?"

I shrugged. "Had a problem with my phone. Did you call me?"

She shook her head. "Mom, I'm going to put Bryce on."

I didn't want to talk, but it was good to hear Mom's voice. Almost soothing. I explained what had happened.

She groaned. "I'm sure the judges will understand."

"You didn't see them," I said. "One guy was about to disqualify me."

"Have you and Ashley seen a lot of each other?"

It was too complicated to get into all that had happened last night, so I just said, "Yeah." Then I told her I was going to take a nap and hung up.

It was clear that Ashley wanted to talk. I tried to listen as she told me about her audition in front of the king of celluloid, but I couldn't concentrate.

"Did Vanessa show up for the audition?" I said.

"No," Ashley said. "It doesn't make sense. You think any of her professors know where she is?"

Just then the back door clicked, and Marion Quidley came running inside. She was out of breath and gasped, "Bryce, you're lucky."

"What?"

"You got third place."

**CHAPTER 31**

✖ Ashley ✖

My first round was ahead, but I had time to go to the academic building where the teachers have offices. We had eaten with Professor Hopper the night before, and I thought he might know Vanessa. I found a directory on the wall and his name under the title Director of Dramatic Arts.

His office was on the third floor, and I took the stairs. There were a couple of office lights on, but most were dark. His door was closed, but beside it was a sign-up sheet for students. Several of the blocks had Vanessa's name.

"You looking for Professor Hopper?" someone said behind me.

I almost jumped out of my skin because I had thought I was alone. I turned and saw Wendell. He had a dust mop in his hands and gave a weird smile. "I clean up part-time. You know, helps pay the college bills."

"Must cost a lot to go here."

He shrugged. "Suppose it'll be worth it if I can get a job, right?" He leaned on the mop handle. "What did you want with Hopper?"

"Vanessa. She wasn't at the audition. Thought he might know something."

Wendell pushed his glasses up with the back of his hand. "She and the prof are pretty close. Seems like every time I come by here they're having a meeting."

"You think there's something going on?"

"He's her adviser. You're supposed to talk as often as you can."

I pointed to the schedule. "Do you meet this much with your adviser?"

He chuckled. "I think I've met with him twice. He has his doubts about whether I should even be enrolled."

"Is there anybody else who might know about Vanessa?"

Someone came out of an office and walked past us.

"Writing people don't mix much with acting people, so I wouldn't know," Wendell said as he pushed the mop down the hall.

# CHAPTER 32

☺ *Bryce* ☺

*I wanted to crawl in bed* and not get up until Sunday, but Kael was there and I asked about his first round.

"Timing was good. Everybody laughed. Good audience. And the judges—"

The phone rang before he could finish. Kael answered and smiled, pumping his fist in the air. "Second place," he said. "We get a first place in the second round, and we'll be in the finals."

I wondered if I even had a chance at the finals with a third-place finish.

Someone knocked on the door, and Kael opened it to find Hunter in full snow gear.

"You guys coming?" he said. "A bunch of us are going to celebrate the end of the first round with a quick trip down the hill. You guys boarders or skiers?"

"Board," Kael said. "I have mine downstairs."

"Ski," I said. "Didn't bring mine."

"That's okay," Hunter said. "A friend left his. I'll bet they'd fit. What size boots you wear?"

I told him.

"Perfect. He's a little guy just like you."

It felt like a slam because I don't see myself as a "little guy."

Kael punched me on the shoulder. "You want to go?"

I stretched, took a look at my bed through the open door, and said, "Yeah, sure."

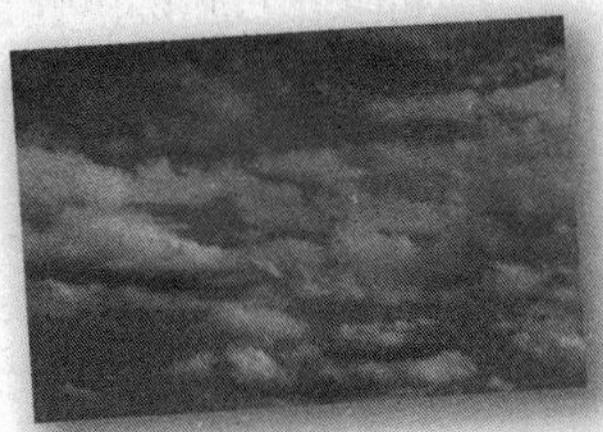

# CHAPTER 33

Ashley

My first round went well—I could hardly top the audition. I got second place and felt that was fair; then I hurried to Marion's competition. I would hate doing an impromptu speech because you have to know a lot about everything.

Here's how it works. A competitor chooses one of three topics, then has seven minutes to respond—usually two minutes to prepare and five minutes to give a speech. You're not supposed to say *uh* and *um,* and what you talk about has to make sense.

In some competitions, I've seen kids fall apart, get stuck, stutter, look at the ceiling, and basically have to sit down in tears.

Marion has blown away the competition in most contests this year. She hasn't finished lower than second in any meet. She comes across as cool, calm, collected, and knowledgeable, which is important. I've seen her talk about everything from term limits for politicians to whether soda should be sold in the hallways of schools.

"You nervous?" I whispered.

She yawned. "I like to go first and put the pressure on the others." Marion's name was sixth out of six.

It made me nervous watching each contestant. Most used note cards to jot down thoughts and get them in order.

The first person chose the topic of whether teachers deserved to be paid according to the grades their students get. The girl speaking said it would be too hard to grade the progress of kids and tie that to the teacher's pay. Plus, she said, some teachers would turn mean toward their students if they did poorly on tests.

Another contestant, a nerdy-looking guy in thick glasses, turned out to be Marion's best competition. His topic was whether America should continue space exploration or use the money to feed the poor. The guy had about 10 examples of inventions and discoveries the space program had provided.

In his summation he said, "It is detrimental to our society to pit space exploration and social problems against each other. Of course we should help feed those who are less fortunate. Our taxes are apportioned for these social problems. But we cannot abandon our interest in space, one of the last frontiers of human exploration. We have no idea what advances await us in medicine, science, and technology. Keep the space program alive."

I looked at Marion and raised my eyebrows. "Pretty good, huh?"

She frowned. "Sounds like he's had that question before."

# CHAPTER 34

☺ *Bryce* ☺

*As we moved downstairs* with our skis and snowboards, others asked us to wait. Hunter just laughed and hung around the lobby. The heat was on high, and I started sweating. Kael phoned Lynette, and she said she'd be down as soon as she found her makeup.

I couldn't believe you needed makeup to go skiing, so I went outside. The boots were a little big, but I had two pairs of socks on to make up the difference.

When everyone was ready, Hunter led us to the rope. Some rode tubes on another hill, but most had snowboards or skis.

Lynette was just ahead of me in a white snowsuit. I don't care how much I didn't like her, seeing her black hair flowing down her back against her pure white suit made me almost lose my balance as I grabbed the rope. Every few minutes, someone would fall, and the person at the top shut the motor off. We'd just hang on until it started again. The experienced skiers were fine, but the beginners flopped like fish out of water.

I made it to the top and adjusted my goggles, then followed Kael and Lynette. The snow was coming down sideways—about two inches had fallen during the day.

Kael and Lynette went over the edge, and I could tell immediately that she knew what she was doing. She wasn't tentative—she leaned forward, wanting speed.

"Scared of the hard skiing?" someone said. It was Hunter, standing by a warning sign. The third slope was roped off.

"We can't go that way."

He lifted the rope. "That was before we got a good snow pack. You want to go?"

The trail headed right into the woods, which I like, but the sign made me nervous. "I've already ticked off my coach. I don't want to do it again."

"I understand." He gave a smarmy smile. "The hill intimidates a lot of people."

I wanted to tell him I'd been skiing since I moved to Colorado, but he took off down the slope, through a grove of trees, and out of sight.

I followed Kael and Lynette.

**CHAPTER 35**

✿ Ashley ✿

When it was Marion's turn, she walked confidently to the front while a judge placed three note cards on the table. To see her concentrate so hard on the topics, then remove two note cards was funny. It was almost like watching a person's brain at work.

She picked up the final card, and a judge started a timer. It made me nervous just watching. Marion looked at the question a long time and finally wrote a few things down. She glanced up at the clock twice, then stepped to the podium, cleared her throat, and looked straight at the audience.

From that moment on, she didn't look at her notes. It was the most incredible thing, like she had a video screen in her head, and she just rattled off the information.

"My topic concerns life on other planets. . . ."

*Oh, my,* I thought. *If the nerdy kid with glasses thought he had his speech memorized, wait until he hears this.*

Marion began with the strange sightings of flying saucers throughout the country over the past 50 years. She talked about actual bodies of aliens captured by the military and documents that she said proved there was a cover-up. Add to that the scores of people who said they had been abducted by aliens, and it felt like one might walk right through the door before she was through.

The kids in the audience hung on every word.

She finished just as the clock clicked to seven minutes, and we knew we were in the presence of someone great. A da Vinci whose canvas was words.

I noticed the kid with thick glasses staring at the wall. When he finally glanced at Marion, he gave a thumbs-up, which I thought showed he was a good sport.

"How do you think you did?" I said.

She shrugged. "Won't know till the judges decide."

"Do you really believe all the stuff you said?"

"You don't have to believe it. You have to convince people of the best arguments either for or against the topic. Of course, it helps if you believe it."

**CHAPTER 36**

☺ *Bryce* ☺

*The ride down the hill was a blast.* I glanced at the path Hunter had taken, but he had disappeared onto a hidden trail.

When I got to the bottom, I found Kael sitting on a bench, Lynette hovering over him. "He twisted his ankle."

"Can you walk?" I said.

"I'm okay. I'm just going back to the room to put some ice on it. I don't want it to swell." He tried to get up, then cried out in pain.

I asked him if he'd heard it crack or anything, and he said he was sure it wasn't broken. I looked around for Hunter. Some RA he was.

"Let's get him back to the room," I said to Lynette.

"No, you two go ahead," Kael said. "I don't want to spoil the fun. There's hardly anybody here."

"Snow's coming down harder," Lynette said. "We shouldn't stay out much longer anyway."

"We won't take no for an answer," I said, kicking off my skis.

Lynette did the same, and we stood on either side of Kael and helped him up.

Once we had him inside, Lynette called her mom, and she met us at our room with a bag of ice. Kael took his boot off, and I examined his ankle. It wasn't swollen and didn't look broken.

After I was sure he was okay, I told Lynette I would get our skis.

"I'll go with you," she said.

Her reaction surprised me. I figured she'd blow me off or let me do it, but she seemed almost eager.

We walked in silence, the falling snow collecting on tree branches above. The sunlight was fading to a soft orange, so everything glowed.

"Beautiful," she said, looking at the mountain and the last of the skiers coming down.

"Yeah." When I'm in the presence of somebody really pretty, I freeze. I worry about stuttering or saying the wrong thing. "You want to take one more run down before we call it a night?"

"Sure," she said.

The wind picked up, and the snow was a white wall in front of us. We stepped into our skis.

"It's gonna feel good to get back and have some hot soup or cocoa after this," she said.

We made our way to the rope and zoomed to the top.

The guy switched the motor off as we caught our balance. "You're the last two tonight. It's turning ugly."

He had a sled that looked like it could go 100 miles an hour. He waved, jumped on the thing, and headed down, disappearing into a white blanket.

I looked at the school but could see only a hazy outline of some lights. The weather had turned so bad that the whole valley was enveloped in snow.

"Amazing, isn't it?" I said.

Lynette nodded, wiping her goggles.

"That's a losing battle," I said.

"Yeah, but I still like to start off with a clean slate."

We stood beside a huge pine tree, partially shielded from the snow. I turned a little so I could look at her face. "I like that too, only with people."

She squinted. "What?"

"A clean slate. Sometimes people get angry at each other, and they spend their whole lives upset when they don't really have to."

She worked on her goggles some more. "Kael says you're a nice guy."

"Well, I'm not going to argue with him. He's right most of the time." I tried to smile, but she wouldn't look up from her goggles. "We got off to a bad start. The whole religion thing—"

The "whole religion thing" (which means that I believe in God and she doesn't) had caused us to argue like rabid coyotes caught in the same trap.

"Does this mean you want to be friends?" she interrupted.

I nodded. "I just can't see going through the next four years of high school being enemies with somebody as . . ." (I wanted to say, "as pretty as you," but I just couldn't bring myself to do it.)

"As what?"

"As talented and smart and . . ."

"Okay, stop," she said, smiling and putting on her goggles. "I'll be honest. I don't think I can ever be friends with somebody like you."

She said it as if I were some kind of mass murderer or a guy who started fires in wilderness areas.

"Well, we can start by going down this hill and seeing where we end up."

She looked at the drifting snow. "I want to do something more challenging. How about you?"

I showed her the closed trail and told her what Hunter had said.

"Let's go down half speed, and tomorrow we'll show that guy who can get down the mountain the fastest."

"I like it." I lifted up the rope and took a look over the edge, the steepest part of the course. "But with this snow, it's going to be kind of hard to—"

Before I could finish, Lynette flew past me and the Keep Out sign, plunging down the trail into the white.

**CHAPTER 37**

✖ Ashley ✖

Word came that Marion had won first place, and I threw my arms around her. "Hail Marion! Queen of Impromptu!"

She frowned and rolled her eyes, but I could tell she enjoyed the attention. She doesn't get that much around school—she just blends into the background—so it was nice to heap some praise on her.

"You're going to Hollywood, no question about it!" I said.

"Won't be any fun unless you go," she said.

I thought about Hayley and wondered how she was doing. Every time I got really excited, the thought of Hayley not being with us made me sad.

"When is your second round?" Marion said.

"Tomorrow morning."

I was getting hungry, and there was a good smell coming from the dining area. I suggested we get something to eat.

As we headed onto the elevator, Lynette's mom got off. "Have you seen my daughter?"

Neither of us had.

"She said she was going for dinner in town," Mrs. Jarvis said to me. "When you see her, tell her to meet me upstairs."

"I'm glad my mom's not here with us," Marion said as we rode downstairs. "It'd be a lot less fun with her watching our every move."

There were only a few people at dinner, and Bryce wasn't one of them. Marion and I went through the line and chose burgers, fries, and salads. Seemed weird, because she always eats healthy stuff.

"It's good to try something different," she said when I stared at her. "Plus, Mom's not here to be the food police."

After we found a table, the Impromptu guy with the thick glasses came up to us. "You were really good today," he said to Marion.

"You too," Marion said. "You got second, right?"

He nodded. "Maybe we'll see each other in the finals."

"Yeah. Good luck."

After he left, I teased Marion and said he was really cute. (He actually wasn't bad-looking, other than the glasses.)

She took a bite of her burger. Finally she said, "I need to talk about something important."

**CHAPTER** 38

☺ *Bryce* ☺

*I regretted our decision* as soon as I got under the rope. Wind howled, and I couldn't see 10 feet in front of me. We get lots of wind where we live, but this was cold, biting, gusty wind that blew snow into my face.

I tried to follow Lynette, but I couldn't even see her tracks. No matter how good she looked in it, it was definitely a mistake to wear a white snowsuit.

My skis swished in the new snow, and the run angled left so much that all I could do was hang on and try to ride it out. The trail dipped, then went back toward a little ridge between some pine trees. As soon as I reached the top, I could see better because the rise blocked the blowing snow. I noticed Lynette's black hair as she glided toward the trees, and my instincts said she was going too fast.

I took off, following her, but she was engulfed in wind and snow. Instead of going straight down the hill to the college, this trail snaked toward the back of the mountain.

I gained speed on another dip and caught up with her at a crest with an orange fence.

"Nice to see you again, pokey," she said.

"We're not going anywhere near the school—"

"You afraid of getting lost?" She shook her head, pulled her goggles down, and took off over the hill.

I wanted to protest, to tell her we should head toward the school, but she was gone.

I followed closely as she navigated another trail that led deeper into the pines. I looked for a familiar landmark, but we were in backcountry. We came to a wooded area, where the trail was so narrow you had to duck because of the limbs. It was nothing but wilderness, spread out in the snowy fog.

Just when I thought we were lost, I saw a light ahead.

Lynette pulled up and waited for me. "You see that?"

"Yeah, keep going."

We got off the main trail and found a smaller one that flattened out and cut through a grove of aspens. In the fall, these turn bright yellow—almost golden in the sunlight. Now they were just white bark. With snow collecting on the barren limbs, the forest looked like a postcard from some resort you see in movies—only we had no idea where the resort was.

My stomach growled because I hadn't eaten much. Skiing, like swimming, makes me hungry. I thought about taking a bite out of an aspen tree but decided to wait.

Lynette pulled up, grabbing a nearby tree. "I don't see the light anymore."

It was definitely getting darker—especially in the woods. I tried to figure out which way was north, but I couldn't because the sun was down.

"Maybe this trail goes to Rocky Mountain National Park," I said. "I noticed on their Web site that they have hiking trails leading there."

"You could get seriously lost in that place," Lynette said.

"What do you want to do?"

The light flashed again.

"Come on!" she said.

# CHAPTER 39

❀ Ashley ❀

Marion looked like someone had stolen her Bigfoot poster.
She always wore a smirk, like life was one big joke, but sitting at the
table with the laughing and talking around us, her face looked less
like a smirk and more like she'd hit a wall head-on, with no helmet.

"What's up?" I said.

She brushed the salt from her hands. "Do you remember your
birthday?"

I remembered it like it was yesterday. Bryce and I had solved a
mystery about a friend of ours that night and had followed another

lead about some money we'd found. All in all, it was a great birthday party.

"Remember when your friend Ruth gave me that pamphlet?"

I'd wanted to forget it. I'd talked with Ruth before the party and told her that Hayley and Marion weren't Christians. I wanted her to be sensitive and not beat them over the head with the Bible. At first, she accused me of being ashamed of the gospel, but finally she decided to attend the party. What I didn't know was that she gave gospel tracts to both Hayley and Marion. They showed me the tracts after Ruth went home.

"Look, I'm really sorry she came on so strong. She can kind of get—"

"That's not my point," Marion said, holding up a greasy hand and stuffing a French fry in her mouth. "I read that pamphlet and looked up the verses in an old Bible."

"And?"

"Well, I'm confused about—"

There was a commotion in the corner as two students from opposing debate teams let their topic spill into the dinner discussion. More people crowded into the room, and it was getting louder.

"Go ahead," I said.

"Well, my problem is, it seems like Christians have to stop thinking and just have faith. You know, throw your brains away and believe."

"That's what some people—"

"I can't throw my brain away, Ashley. I mean, God coming to earth and sacrificing his life for us is compelling, but there are just so many things . . ." Her voice trailed off as some kids threw food.

"You want to get out of here and take a walk?" I said.

"I'd love it."

**CHAPTER 40**

☺ *Bryce* ☺

*Lynette and I moved toward the light,* winding around some huge pine trees and trying to stay on a path. The farther we went, the more uneasy I felt. I've read stories of people getting caught in an avalanche or taking a wrong turn in the snow and getting lost. At best, the people lost toes and fingers to frostbite. At worst, they died.

I remembered the verse in the Bible that talks about Satan disguising himself as an "angel of light," and that got me even more scared. As we slowly skied into the wilderness, I prayed for wisdom.

Some people "say" a prayer, as if all you have to do is mouth the words. I *prayed*, as in, if we didn't get help from God we were going to be royally cold as ice cubes before this was over.

*Please, God,* I prayed, *you know everything. You know exactly where we are and what it will take to get us out of this mess. I don't want a big rescue party coming up here looking for us, but we need your help. Show us the right path, and if this light is not what we should follow, show us that too.* I prayed for both of us because I knew Lynette was not the praying type.

"You getting cold?" she called.

"I was cold when I got out here," I said. "I'm okay, though. You?"

"My face is numb. And I can't feel my fingertips."

"Hold up," I said.

I looked closely at her face. Her nose was red and so were her cheeks. I couldn't help noticing how dark her eyebrows were, and her eyes were like . . . well, I'll spare you the details, but believe me, she's pretty even when she's freezing. I took off the scarf I was wearing.

She protested. "You don't have to do that."

"I know. But you're a lot colder than I am."

I put the scarf around her neck, making sure it covered her face but that she could still see. "That better?"

"Yeah." She looked down. "You think we're lost?"

"I'm not sure we're going in the right direction, and it bugs me that we can't see the town."

"You want to turn back?"

"We've twisted and turned so much—I don't know if we'd find our way. Plus, the snow's coming down so hard our tracks are covered."

Her teeth chattered, and she rubbed her gloves together. "I'm getting hungry. And I haven't had much to drink. They say you can really get dehydrated out here."

That was a problem. Eating snow would cure the dehydration, but it would also make us colder.

"It's up to you," she said. "I'm out of ideas."

"Let's keep going."

# CHAPTER 41

✖ Ashley ✖

Marion and I checked with Mr. Gminski before leaving, and he said we could take a walk. The snow was pretty, and the streetlights made everything glow. We walked along the road leading toward the little town, and I suggested we find a coffee shop. Marion said that would be great.

"So let me get this right," I began when we were alone. "You're afraid the Christian stuff will make you leave your brain on the shelf and just believe something because you're supposed to?"

"Yeah, basically. Take the whole Adam-and-Eve thing. Or Noah's Flood. From what I read, if you don't believe they're literally true, you can't be a Christian—at least not your brand of Christian."

I didn't like the your-brand-of-Christian line, but I tried not to let it show.

"And the miracles of Jesus. You know, raising the dead. Healing the sick. They're all nice stories, and they inspire, but how can a thinking person believe them?"

"What if they actually happened?" That stopped her. We were crossing a little bridge over a creek. "I mean, take the story of Jesus in the boat."

"The walking-on-the-water thing?" she said.

"Yeah. It's hard to believe someone actually walked on water. It's a physical impossibility, right?"

"Unless there were stones underneath and he knew where he was going," Marion said.

I gave her a look and pointed at the creek. "No, imagine a lake that's really deep and has rough water. The wind is howling. You're in this little boat, and you're scared to death that you're going to capsize and drown. And all of a sudden here comes this guy walking on the waves. You can't believe it."

"Right. I can't."

We started walking again.

"Well, you're in good company, because the guys who were there couldn't believe it either. That's one of the things that lets me know the Bible is true. The disciples were really scared, and they didn't even recognize Jesus when he came to them. If it had been me writing it, I probably would have fudged and said, 'We were scared, but we realized it was Jesus all along.' The Bible is totally honest like that. You see people's warts and all. Jesus picked a lot of sinners to follow him."

"So how is that supposed to help me believe?" Marion said.

I turned toward her. "God doesn't ask you to believe in something he's not willing to show. In other words, anybody could say they're God, that they come from God, and that if you believe they're the real thing it's all good, you'll go to heaven. End of story."

"As long as you give money to their church," Marion said, smiling.

"Yeah. But God never asks anybody to believe something he's not willing to prove. Jesus didn't raise people from the dead in secret; he did it in front of people. When he healed, he did it out in the open. When he rose from the dead, he came and talked with people—hundreds, in fact. And the great thing is . . ."

"The great thing is what?" she said. "What are you looking at?"

We had moved along the street to a bunch of shops. I realized the one we were standing in front of was the very store where Vanessa worked.

**CHAPTER 42**

☺ *Bryce* ☺

*Lynette and I dodged trees and rocks,* moving slowly along the trail. I knew it was dangerous because one wrong turn could prove disastrous.

I thought about Ashley and wondered if she'd notice that I was gone. Some people think twins have this inner sense when something's wrong with their sibling, but I think that's a bunch of hooey. I've been in scrapes where I could have been really hurt, and Ashley was doing her nails or washing her hair.

Suddenly everything changed. And not for the better. The wind had been howling, the snow pelting us so hard that I could hear the pitter-patter against my coat. Now the wind sounded like a freight train, blowing so hard against our faces that I had to look sideways just to breathe. It stung, like someone had aimed a snow cannon at us.

Lynette turned. "I have to stop."

We took off our skis and propped them by a tree, then found shelter behind it, blocking the wind. I went through my pockets and found a small granola bar—chocolate chip and peanut butter—and gave it to Lynette. She gobbled it down without even offering me half.

I tried my cell phone a few times, but there was no signal. "Someone will come for us," I said.

"When?" she yelled. "I told my mom I was going into town for dinner—I didn't want to eat in the dining hall. She probably thinks that's where we are."

"Even though you hate me?"

She didn't answer. She just pulled her arms into her coat and tried to get warm.

"The best way to go is down," I said, getting as close as I dared. "We keep walking around up here and we'll fall."

"How can you go down when you can't see?"

"I'll hang on to trees until—"

"Look!" she shouted.

The light again. It was blurry in the snow and flickering below us on what looked like another trail. Just as soon as we'd seen it, it went out.

"Come on!" Lynette jumped up and headed toward the light.

# CHAPTER 43

❀ Ashley ❀

I didn't want to interrupt the most important conversation I'd ever had with Marion, but the dress shop took my breath away. It was still light inside, and the Open sign was in the front door.

I turned to Marion. "Some of the smartest people in the world have believed in Christianity. One guy I read about was a journalist. He'd won awards writing for the *Chicago Tribune,* and he set out to write a book disproving everything the Bible said."

"What happened?"

"He became a Christian. It was the first time in his life that he gave the Bible a chance, that he really read it. He thought God was a crutch, made up by people trying to solve their problems."

Marion nodded.

"I felt the same way," I said. "I thought my mom was joining a church to get over my dad's death and that her marriage to Sam wasn't what she'd hoped. But when I listened to the message—I mean, really listened with an open mind—it all made sense. If God doesn't exist, we're on our own and there's really no purpose to life. But if God does exist, if he made the universe and all humans, he must have some purpose for us."

Suddenly I thought about Hayley. If she were here I knew that Marion and I wouldn't be having this conversation. In a million years I hadn't thought Marion would be open to talking about spiritual stuff because she'd been so sarcastic about church and the Bible, but here we were.

Marion was deep in thought. I had laid out some serious stuff—not in detail, but that could wait. If she wanted specifics, I would give them, but I didn't want to overload her.

A horn honked, and we turned as a car slid into another car on the slick road. We grabbed our ears just before the sickening impact. The guy in the rear car got out and immediately fell. It would have been funny if it hadn't been so serious.

A girl from the dress shop came out, then rushed back inside to the phone.

"You want to go in?" I said.

"Yeah, I need to think awhile and get warm," Marion said.

**CHAPTER 44**

☺ *Bryce* ☺

*Lynette and I left our skis* and walked carefully down, grabbing one tree at a time. I'd read a true story about some people climbing Mount Everest. A storm pounded the group, and one guy got separated. He decided to stop and wait until morning. When the sun came up, he was nearly frozen and just a few feet from a drop that would have killed him.

I doubted Lynette had read any stories like that, because she was moving fast. When you're cold and wet and hungry and tired (plus, you have to go to the bathroom and can't tell the girl you're with), you don't think about why there's a light out there—you just follow it.

We both yelled, thinking whoever had the light would stop and show us how to get back to the school, but all we could see was a wall of snow.

I got in front of Lynette and forced her to move slower. We hit a grove of pines so thick that it blocked some of the wind, but as soon as we were out, we got pelted again.

For a moment, there was a break in the wind, and I looked down the mountain. Nothing but wilderness. I tried to tell Lynette.

She pushed past me. "This has to be the way. We both saw the light."

"Maybe it was a mirage. Maybe a reflection of some shooting star on the snow or an optical illusion. Lynette, we have to go back up the hill to our—"

"There!" she shouted. "Look!"

I squinted into the swirling snow and spotted a dull, flickering light. My heart jumped when I saw smoke rising.

In the middle of the wilderness, on what looked like the edge of the world, there was a cabin with a fire going.

# CHAPTER 45

❦ Ashley ❦

Melanie's was a quaint store with dresses and sweaters on racks and jeans and pants stacked on shelves. The store was narrow and long, and the cash register was in the back. Marion and I wiped our feet on a mat and tried not to track snow on the shiny hardwood floor, but we had so much snow on us that we dripped.

The girl at the register waved us back, telling us with a smile that it was okay as she talked with the police. When she hung up, she moved toward us, looking out the window. "It's going to be tough tonight. There's already a bunch of accidents."

"We walked up from the school, and it's really nasty," I said.

"You must be in for the speech tournament," she said. I was close enough now to see her name badge. It said *Rhonda*.

I told her our names and that we were from Red Rock.

"Long way to come for a tournament," Rhonda said. "You like the school?"

I nodded. "What I really want to know about is another girl who works here. Do you know Vanessa Harvey?"

She smirked. "Yeah. I'm working for her tonight."

"Really? Did she ask you?"

"No, the owner called and said she didn't show up for her shift this evening. But she's usually on time for everything."

Marion wandered off and looked at some jeans and sweaters.

I took the opportunity to question Rhonda. "That's weird because Vanessa was supposed to go to an audition today."

"She didn't show up?" Rhonda said. "That *is* strange. The audition was all she talked about the past couple of weeks. How she wanted to get out of here, be an actress and all that."

"What do you think happened?"

Rhonda shrugged. "Beats me. She's kind of been in her own little world. You know, talking about the play she's in, the audition, what she'd do if she gets the part, and stuff about her boyfriend."

"She has a boyfriend?"

Rhonda laughed. "She probably has a bunch lining up at her door, but she only talked about one guy."

"What's his name?"

"She never told me. It was kind of her little secret. I figured it was some professor's son or something like that. But he's definitely a student at CSD."

*Great. That narrows things down.* "Do you think she would have run off with him?" I said. "Maybe gone home or to his house?"

"She wouldn't have missed that audition for anything."

"Does she have any enemies?" I said, remembering Vanessa's diary and what she'd written about Jen.

"I suppose everybody she's competing against at that school is her enemy. Vanessa is not the warm, fuzzy type. She knows what she wants and tries to get it. Know what I mean?"

"I'm in middle school. It's my life."

Marion snickered behind us.

"Right," Rhonda said. "How do you know so much about Vanessa?"

I briefly told her I was staying in her room and had become concerned about her. Security had located her car but not her.

Rhonda bit her lip. "She was supposed to stay with me this week. But she didn't show last night. Didn't even call."

"Can you think of anything she said or did that was out of the ordinary lately?"

"She's not the hiking or wilderness type, you know. Manicured nails. Nice clothes. Perfect hair. Doesn't ski or anything. But last week, she bought this huge parka. I asked her what it was for, and she got mad at me. Next time I saw her she acted like nothing had happened."

**CHAPTER** 46

☺ *Bryce* ☺

*Lynette and I clomped through the snow* in our boots, finding a couple of unexpected rocks. As we neared the cabin, it became clear that this was no chalet. No electric lines and I guessed no phone either. Just a stack of firewood covered with snow. The place looked a hundred years old.

"Hello?" Lynette yelled as we came closer.

A wave of wind swept over the house, and I shook the snow off my hat and knocked on the door. "Hello? We need some help."

There was only one window in the front, and it was covered with snow.

"There has to be someone in there," Lynette said, shivering. "Someone had to start that fire."

"Unless they're still out here," I said. "Maybe the person with the light."

"I thought that was a mirage," Lynette said.

There was no doorknob, just a wooden latch on a metal hinge with a hole for a combination lock, but it was empty. I lifted the latch and a blast of warm air hit us. I pushed Lynette forward and closed the door behind us. We pulled off our gloves, got on our knees, and held our bare hands out toward the fire. The wood was fresh.

I looked around the room. No water faucet, no refrigerator. There was a table and four chairs—all crude.

Lynette edged closer to the fire. By now I *really* had to go to the bathroom and excused myself and walked outside. People joke about boys writing their names in the snow, but I felt like I could have written the preamble to the constitution.

As I turned to go inside, Lynette appeared at the door, her eyes as wide as soccer balls. "You'd better come see this."

# CHAPTER 47

❀ Ashley ❀

Marion and I walked back to the college, and I could tell she was
still thinking. Cars and trucks slid all over the streets. One car had
plunged into the creek.

We looked for Bryce in the lobby of Harris Hall, where kids practiced their routines while others played games. Someone had
brought a tray with cookies, juice, and soda. I was surprised Bryce
wasn't in the middle of the party because he has a nose for food.

We rode the elevator up and knocked on his door. Mr. Gminski
opened it. Kael sat with his leg propped up on a pillow. He told us his
story, and I asked where Bryce was.

"Last I saw him, he and Lynette were going back for their skis," Kael said.

Lynette's mother came in, her face tight. "Where's your brother?"

"I was just looking for him," I said. I picked up the phone and dialed his cell number. The call immediately went to Bryce's answering system, which meant the phone was off or out of range. "Bryce, it's Ashley. Where are you? Is Lynette with you? No matter where you are, call us."

"Give him my cell number," Lynette's mom said.

I repeated the number she gave and hung up.

I followed Lynette's mom to the elevator and noticed that the RA's door was open. Jen was inside, crying.

"What's up?" I said.

She wiped her eyes, looking out the window. "I just heard back about the audition. They didn't pick any of us."

"That's too bad." I put a hand on her shoulder. "Why are you up here?"

"This is my boyfriend's room. Hunter usually helps me through the bad times, but—"

A tall guy wearing ski pants and covered in snow appeared at the door. He shed his jacket and hat and hugged Jen.

"I didn't get called," Jen sobbed.

He pursed his lips and looked at me. "Mind if we talk?"

"No problem," I said. "You don't know where Bryce is, do you?"

"He's not here?" Hunter said. "I haven't seen him for a couple of hours."

# CHAPTER 48

◒ *Bryce* ◒

**There was another room** to the cabin—a bedroom—and the door was open. I peeked in and saw a candle glowing by a single bed. No mirror. No dresser. There were tiny holes in the wall, and snow drifted through. On the bed was a big lump under some covers.

"Is he . . . or she . . . alive?" I said.

"I don't know," Lynette said. "I was looking for something to drink and found . . . it."

This room was a lot colder. Leaves and pine needles collected in a corner. I thought I saw something move in the flickering light and wondered if mice lived at this altitude.

"Find any water?" I said.

"I had a little from an open bottle near the fire," Lynette said. "It was all I could find, but it tasted weird." She moved closer. "What do we do?"

I took a breath, then walked loudly to the bed and picked up the candle. It was a big candle in a glass jar, the kind Ashley likes. I held it out and reached for the top cover.

Suddenly someone sat straight up. It was a dark-haired female. She took in a gulp of air, coughed, and squinted. "Who are you?"

"Bryce, and this is Lynette. We got lost and found your cabin. Who are you?"

"Vanessa Harvey." She pulled the covers back and stood. She wore a gargantuan parka and had a hard time getting her balance. She put a hand to her head and the other on the bed to steady herself.

"How long have you been here?" I said.

"I'm not sure. Last thing I remember . . . oh, I think I'm going to be sick."

I grabbed a plastic bucket from the other room and handed it to her. She lay back on the bed and put a hand over her forehead.

"Were you skiing up here?" Lynette said.

"No, the last thing I remember is coming home from work. I got out of my car, and somebody jumped me. When I woke up, I was here."

"Have you eaten anything? had anything to drink?" I said.

"Just the water in there and some really nasty stuff in a plastic bag." She stood again. "Every time I get up, things get blurry."

Lynette put a hand on her stomach. "I'm not feeling very good either."

"That water must have something in it. Something to keep you knocked out."

"Great," Lynette said.

I found a couple of tin cups, scooped some snow outside, and put the cups by the fireplace. "As soon as we have some clean water, you can drink it."

Lynette sat at the table, her head in her hands. Vanessa was still wobbly.

"Did you see who jumped you?" I said.

Vanessa shook her head. "Must have been a guy. He was really strong."

If he had carried her from Tres Peaks, he had to be as strong as the Hulk. I couldn't imagine anyone being able to do that, unless he used a sled. And wouldn't someone have seen him?

"Do you know where you are?" I said.

She shook her head. I told her about the light and she gasped. "That guy might be on his way back here."

**CHAPTER 49**

✖ Ashley ✖

Marion and I stuck together, asking everybody about Bryce. He wasn't in the dorm. I tried his phone again but got his voice mail.

Mr. Gminski grilled me, and I assured him that I didn't know anything. Lynette's mom called campus security and the police.

Someone turned up the television in the lobby just as the weather guy broke in with a bulletin. ". . . situation is critical tonight. Especially vulnerable is this area from Boulder all the way up to Tres Peaks. This area could be hit with 30 inches or more of snow before Sunday. As you can see, this system is quite strong and could result in significant snowfall in the next 24 to 48 hours."

I thought about calling Mom to ask if Bryce had phoned her, but the last thing I wanted to do was needlessly scare her.

I broke away from the group and ran upstairs. I closed the door to my room and jumped onto the bed, covering my face with my hands.

*God,* I prayed, *you know where Bryce is and if he's okay. Please help us find him or have him call us and tell us where he is. If he's in some kind of trouble, give him a clear mind. Help him think through everything.*

A tear leaked out of one eye, and I brushed it away. *Lord Jesus, I don't know where Lynette is either. Maybe they're together. You know how much she and her family hate people who talk about you. If she's somehow involved, if she's tried to hurt Bryce . . . please keep them safe and help us find them before this storm gets worse.*

# CHAPTER 50

☺ Bryce ☺

**I found a fireplace poker** and kept it handy in case the guy came back. I also put a few chairs in front of the door so we'd have warning.

I had Lynette drink some of the melted snow. It seemed to help a little. I also found a plastic bag in the corner and opened it. Inside were cans of vegetables, soup, beef jerky, and SPAM. Some of it you had to heat up, so I gave the girls a choice between jerky and SPAM. They both gagged at the jerky.

I'd done a report about SPAM in history class, believe it or not. The canned meat was actually used to feed soldiers in World War II.

Because of the way it was packed, it kept for years without refrigeration. It really was a miracle meat to those guys.

I don't mean to offend anyone who likes it, but the smell reminded me of dog food. There was a gelatin film all around the meat, like a dog had slobbered on it. I pulled it out, scraped the gelatin off, and cut a slice with my pocketknife.

Lynette looked at it like it was a piece of my small intestine. I guess I couldn't blame her. I cut another piece for Vanessa, then one for me. Both of them just stared at it.

"Well, cheers," I said, taking a big bite and acting like it was prime rib. I was so hungry I could have eaten tree bark, but I had to admit the SPAM had a salty, hamlike taste. "Hey, not bad."

Lynette tried some, then Vanessa. It was clear that neither of them cared for it, but they both knew they had to eat something. I've seen people eat sheep's eyes and bugs the size of your hand on those TV shows that dare you to do something stupid, so this was a breeze.

I cut a stick from a tree outside, sharpened the end, and stuck a piece of SPAM on it. I held it in the fire for a few seconds, heating it up.

"From what I told you about our skiing, do you have any idea where we are?" I said to Vanessa.

"Yeah. I think I do. I've never been here, but I've heard of this place. There's a few of them around."

"A few what?" Lynette said.

"Emergency shelters," Vanessa said. "They were built for hikers and skiers who get lost. At least that's what they said in one of my classes. They were supposed to be stocked with provisions for a few days and matches for a fire."

"Sure came in handy for us," Lynette said.

"Why would they have a lock?" I said.

Vanessa shrugged. "I heard some kids were hanging out here in the summer, so they locked them until winter."

I cut some more SPAM, but they didn't want any. I ate theirs, put the rest in the can, and covered it.

The girls were huddled by the fireplace, so I pulled a chair close. "Who would want to do this to you?" I said.

"Honestly, I don't know."

"You said the guy grabbed you after work. That was Tuesday, right?"

"Tuesday . . ." A look of horror came over her. "What day is this? It's Wednesday, isn't it? Please tell me it's Wednesday."

I shook my head. "Actually it's Thursday."

"The audition!" Vanessa cried. "I missed the audition!"

**CHAPTER 51**

❀ Ashley ❀

I was still praying when the door to the room squeaked. I turned and saw Marion. She kind of smiled, then sat on the bed.

"Any word yet?" I said.

"Not yet. The security guys are out checking the campus. You okay?"

I nodded. "Just doing the best thing I can do."

"What's that?"

"I know somebody who cares even more than I do about Bryce and Lynette. I was just talking to him."

Marion bit her cheek. "You think God—if he exists—cares for

people who don't like him? Or who seem to be against him, like Lynette?"

"God cares for everybody. The Bible says that he doesn't want anyone to die without coming to know him . . . or something like that. If anyone is sorry for the wrong things they've done and asks forgiveness, God promises he will forgive. Simple as that."

"Don't you have to promise you'll go to church or give 10 percent of your income?"

I laughed. "Yeah, as soon as you ask forgiveness, you have to sign a binding contract that falls out of heaven."

Marion looked away.

"It was just funny sounding; that's all."

Before I could say anything else, the door flew open and Lynette's mother ran in. A security guard was with her—one of the same guys who had taken us to Vanessa's car the night before.

"This is his sister. I think she knows what that boy did with my daughter."

"What?" I said.

"We almost put a restraining order on him earlier this year," Lynette's mom said. "He was making threats."

"I can't believe you think Bryce—"

"He planned this whole thing, and I wouldn't be surprised if she knows about it."

Marion stood. I sat up and looked at the security guy.

"Well?" he said. "Do you know where they are?"

**CHAPTER 52**

☺ *Bryce* ☺

*I was a lot less concerned* about a dumb old audition than about getting home alive. If no one found us, we'd have to live on SPAM. Plus, a kidnapper was out there.

Lynette tried to calm Vanessa, but her emotions sent her over the edge. I was afraid the crying would bring the kidnapper back or the SPAM would lure some wild animals. I checked the door and scraped the window as best I could, but I didn't see any movement outside.

Finally Vanessa's crying turned into sniffles and snorts.

I put the last piece of wood in the fire and told them I was going for more.

"Don't go, Bryce," Lynette said.

"That fire goes out and we're in big trouble. I saw a stack by the cabin. I won't be long."

"Be careful," Vanessa said.

The wind blew hard as I pushed the door open. I kicked some of the snow out of the way and got it closed. This was not the powdery Colorado snow that melts fast. It was heavy, wet, and hard to walk through.

I wished I had a flashlight or a lantern because I couldn't see. I used the side of the cabin to guide me and found the stack of firewood. I brushed off the snow and gathered an armload.

On my third trip outside, I heard something move near the cabin. "Hello?" I yelled.

I looked for any light, any movement, but a guy could have been standing a yard away from me and I wouldn't have seen him.

"I've got a weapon," I shouted.

Nothing.

Then I heard it again—a whomp—and I realized the trees were losing clumps of snow.

I prayed, asking God to help us get out alive; then I remembered our youth pastor. During Sunday school he said that everything happens for a reason, and God can use even the bad stuff to bring him glory.

It made me wonder if Lynette or Vanessa might be interested in spiritual stuff. I prayed God would help me speak openly and honestly about him.

"Is it letting up at all?" Vanessa said when I got the door closed.

Lynette didn't even look up. She could tell by all the snow that had blown in.

"Still coming down hard, but if we can make it through the night, we'll be all right."

"How do you figure that?" Vanessa said. "We're miles from any-body, and they'd never be able to get back here."

I turned on my cell phone. I had plenty of power, but there was no signal. "If the weather breaks in the morning, I'll climb up and get a signal."

# CHAPTER 53

Ashley

The security guy took me to the lobby, away from everyone, and sat me in an overstuffed chair by the fireplace. "You want something to drink?"

I shook my head. "I don't know what happened. I've been looking like everybody else."

He held up a hand and knelt on one knee. "Let's start at the beginning. Is it true your brother was harassing this girl?"

I tried to explain what had happened, that Lynette was an atheist or agnostic or whatever and she'd been offended when anyone talked about God. I told him about the climbing wall built in honor of our friend Jeff and that Lynette had complained and had it taken down.

"So there is a reason for your brother to be mad at her."

"Yeah, but . . . no. He just tries to stay out of her way."

"Her mother said she came here to protect her daughter from your brother."

"That's nonsense. Bryce is a nice guy. There's a better chance that Lynette did something to him than the other way around."

"I've seen your brother. He's big enough to push somebody off a cliff, don't you think?"

I clenched my teeth. "My brother would never hurt anyone. You should be out there looking for him."

The radio squawked. The guard stood and headed to the next room. "Yeah, go ahead."

Jen walked into the room and sat down. "You okay?" she said.

I nodded. "They think my brother is a stalker, but they're wrong." I wanted to ask Jen about Vanessa's diary and what it said about her, but Lynette's mom ran into the room. Before she could speak, I said, "Mrs. Jarvis, Bryce would never hurt Lynette. He actually kind of likes her."

"People can put on a good act. They plan things and—" She stopped as the security guy came back into the room.

"There's been an accident just outside town," he said.

"An accident?" Mrs. Jarvis said.

"A young guy and a girl are trapped in the backseat. They fit the descriptions of your daughter and your brother."

"Take me there," Mrs. Jarvis said.

**CHAPTER** 54

◐ *Bryce* ◐

*After we stacked the wood,* we pulled the mattress near the
fire. The girls grabbed blankets while I put the box spring nearby.

Lynette handed me a blanket, and I took my boots off and tried to
get my feet warm. Every time I'd try to get closer to the fire, the
springs would creak and the sound made Lynette and Vanessa laugh.
I heard on some radio show that laughing does something in your
body and can warm you. I figured it was worth trying.

I told them all the jokes I knew, and Lynette threw in a couple.

When we ran out of material, Vanessa chimed in with a section
she had memorized from her play. The fire danced in her eyes and
her hair shone as she went into "acting" mode. I could tell she was

really good, and I understood why she was so disappointed about missing the audition.

I put a slightly wet piece of wood on the fire, and it crackled, popped, and smoked. I didn't want to use too much wood too fast, but it was getting colder.

"We should tell our life stories," Vanessa said. "You first, Lynette. Did you grow up in Colorado?"

Lynette shook her head and told us where she was born, a little about her father and mother, and how they had moved to Wyoming to get back to nature. A land battle sent them packing to Red Rock.

"Do you like the new place?" Vanessa said.

"We've adjusted. I have a horse and get to ride him a lot."

"And you like the speech team?" Vanessa said.

Lynette looked at me. "For the most part."

"What about you?" I said to Vanessa.

"I grew up in Denver and stayed there till I was 10. My parents split, and I moved to California with my mom. That was hard. Dad stayed in Colorado. When I graduated high school, I applied to CSD."

"Is that what you want to do, act?" Lynette said.

"Oh yeah." Vanessa smiled, and it looked like an orthodontist's dream. I could imagine her on a poster outside theaters. "Since I was little I've been making my own movies. It really is my passion."

She told us about the plays she'd been in and that she'd starred in a toilet-paper commercial (which I thought was funny) and been an extra in a movie. She had her career planned—act, make money, then direct and produce.

"Do you have a boyfriend?" Lynette said.

Vanessa smiled again. "Yeah. He's into filmmaking too."

She wouldn't tell us his name. Finally, after some insights on her acting theory, she turned to me. "What about you, Brent?"

**CHAPTER 55**

❀ Ashley ❀

Lynette's mom and I jumped into the security guard's four-wheel-drive vehicle. Mr. Gminski came with us. I used the guard's mobile phone to dial Mom and Sam. It was the hardest call I've ever had to make.

The security guard took the phone and told them the mountain pass had been closed. I guessed Sam wanted to fly up because the guard mentioned that the closest airport had also been closed.

"We'll keep you informed," the guard said.

The windshield wipers beat to the tune of some sad country song. It felt like we were on our way to a funeral. We came upon the eerie glow of flashing yellow-and-red lights.

"Looks like they're still trying to get them out," the guard said as he stopped. "Wait right here."

"Why would Bryce and Lynette be out here?" I said, looking at the curvy two-lane road.

"Maybe they got lost," Mr. Gminski said. "Someone passing could have offered a ride—"

"But Bryce would have called," I said.

Mr. Gminski opened the door and stepped out. "I'm going to check on them."

I heard an engine spark to life, and firemen moved around the crashed car. Soon our windshield was covered with snow.

I looked at Mrs. Jarvis and said a prayer for both of us.

**CHAPTER 56**

☻ *Bryce* ☻

*Vanessa had called me Brent,* but I didn't correct her. Of course, if I saved her life and she became a star, I'd want her to mention her Colorado friend by name and invite me to the premiere.

I told Vanessa and Lynette about growing up near Chicago, watching the Bears and the Cubs. When I told them about my real dad and what happened to him, all you could hear was the fire crackling.

Then I explained how we had moved to Colorado and that my mom had gotten religious. "Ashley and I thought she was going to church only because our real dad went a lot. Finally we started going ourselves and found out it's different than the weird stuff you see on TV."

*Snap. Crackle. Pop.*

It sounded more like a Rice Krispies convention. I wanted both of them to see the fire inside me, that God was real and wanted a relationship with them. I imagined the three of us holding hands and praying.

"So you bought the same stuff your mom did, huh?" Lynette said.

I looked at her, my mouth open in an *O*. I could see my breath as I exhaled. "In a way, I guess." I left it at that because if people want to know more, they usually ask questions.

Vanessa smiled nervously. "Well, anybody know a ghost story?"

**CHAPTER 57**

❀ Ashley ❀

The EMTs had the driver of the car on a stretcher when Mrs. Jarvis and I approached. Others worked on the back door that had been smashed by a tree. The firemen used a machine that pried the door open. When they moved in, I held my breath.

I closed my eyes and prayed, but I couldn't help thinking of Dad's funeral and what Mom would look like standing by Bryce's casket. How would we explain all this to Dylan? Tears came to my eyes.

Mrs. Jarvis gasped as the firemen pulled a young lady from the car. "That's not Lynette," she whispered.

A guy was next—he was talking and moving his arms.

"Do you recognize them?" the security guard said.

Mrs. Jarvis shook her head.

"Are they going to be all right?" I said.

"All three are alive," he said. "They're headed to the hospital."

**CHAPTER 58**

☾ *Bryce* ☾

*Instead of ghost stories,* Vanessa and Lynette sang a bunch of songs. I didn't recognize any of them. Then another thump sounded outside, and a big one hit the roof. I scratched a hole in the ice on the window and saw a drift of snow several feet deep.

I went back to the fire, where Lynette and Vanessa had suddenly become old pals. I was officially the odd man out.

When the concert was over, I jumped in with a question for Vanessa. "What if the person who brought you up here wanted you gone during the audition?"

"You mean one of the other girls?" Vanessa said.

"Yeah, to get you out of the way."

"I suppose it could happen." Vanessa had been lying on her side, propped up by an elbow. Now she snapped to attention. "I hadn't thought of that. You think somebody would go that far?"

"What girl would be strong enough to grab you, then drag you up here?" Lynette said. "Seems far-fetched."

"Maybe she hired somebody," I said. "A boyfriend or some guy she promised big money to if she got the part."

Except for the wind, the room was quiet.

"There's the RA on our floor," Vanessa said. "Her name's Jen. We've kind of butted heads recently."

"She's got big muscles," Lynette said.

"Does Jen have a boyfriend?" I said.

"She's dating another RA. Hunter something."

"Whoa," I said, flabbergasted. "Hunter is the one who tried to get me to go onto the advanced trail. He could have been the one with the flashlight—"

"Advanced trail?" Vanessa said. "There's no such thing. They have a cross-country trail that winds around the mountain and then heads this way, but that's closed."

"He told me it was the advanced trail," I said. My mind spun with ideas. "If those two are involved, they won't want anybody snooping around trying to figure it out." I pulled out my cell phone.

"What are you doing?" Vanessa said.

"Trying to call my sister. Once she discovers we're missing, she's bound to look for clues."

The cell phone still didn't get a signal. I looked out the window again, praying the snow would let up.

It just kept getting worse.

# CHAPTER 59

✖ Ashley ✖

I called Mom on the way back to the dorm and told her the good news. She seemed relieved, but I could tell we were both thinking the same thing. If Bryce wasn't in the car and he hadn't called, something was really wrong.

Jen's boyfriend, Hunter, asked to speak with Mr. Gminski in private. When our teacher came back, I asked what Hunter wanted.

"He feels bad about challenging Bryce to go down a cross-country slope."

"Bryce took him up on it?"

"No. To his credit, he didn't take the dare, so Hunter went down a different way. I just spoke with the young man operating the rope lift. He said there were two kids—a guy and a girl—at the top when he left. He didn't see either of them come down."

I scratched my head. "So Lynette follows Bryce, or the other way around, and they get turned around or disoriented in the snow...."

Someone behind me cleared his throat. I turned and saw Wendell.

"There's a bunch of old cabins scattered around the mountain," he said. "If they got caught in this, they probably holed up in one of them and made a fire."

Hunter came toward us. "I think we should try to find them."

"In this?" Wendell said.

I checked the forecast on the Internet. More bad news. Worst storm in 50 years—if it kept up. People stranded. Emergency vehicles stuck.

A security guard walked up to us. "We have a couple of snowmobiles in storage. We'll crank them up in the morning, but no one is going out tonight."

I retreated to my room to think. What if this wasn't an accident? What if Bryce and Lynette had been attacked by some maniac? If Vanessa had been attacked, had the guy struck again?

# CHAPTER 60

☺ *Bryce* ☺

*I awoke and sat up* on the box spring. Was that a face at the window? Big, bushy eyebrows and a scary-looking nose? I rubbed my eyes and looked again. Had I dreamed it?

I checked my watch, pushing the Light button and watching the blue-green glow. Vanessa and Lynette had stretched out in opposite directions on the mattress and were sound asleep.

I added wood to the fire to keep the room warm and watched the snow push through a hole in the wall. I got enough courage to walk to the window and look outside. Nothing.

I took a walk into the bedroom. It was pitch-black and 15 degrees cooler inside. By punching my watch I was able to see a little. I found the candle and used a small piece of wood to light it.

The bed had wooden slats, and I figured we could use those if we ran out of firewood. I knelt on the cold wooden floor and set the candle down. Under the bed, shoved against the wall, was a green backpack—the kind you find in an army-surplus store.

I grabbed it and lifted the crumbling leather flap. To my surprise, I found more SPAM, a few cans of beans, a can opener, some bottled water, and a black radio with a long antenna.

I hunkered down in the corner and turned on the radio. It squawked.

"Mayday, Mayday," I said in a hoarse whisper. I've always wanted to say that. "Can anybody hear me?"

I let go of the button and listened. I repeated my Mayday, and when no one answered, I went to the next channel. I was on channel 27 when the door opened.

"What are you doing?" Vanessa said.

"I found this under the bed."

"A walkie-talkie?" she said, her eyes wide. "Maybe someone will hear us!"

**CHAPTER 61**

✾ Ashley ✾

It was the longest night of my life. I was so tired, but every time I
put my head down, I thought of Bryce in the blizzard, frozen to a
tree or at the bottom of an icy pond.

Mrs. Jarvis paced the living room, and when she wasn't doing
that she was in the hall talking with Jen or downstairs on the phone
with her husband. He had tried to get to us but had to turn back because I-25 was closed.

There were no weather updates, but every time I looked out the
window I saw steady snow.

At 5:30 a.m. a security guard knocked on our door. "We got a call on our emergency frequency a few minutes ago. I think you should hear this." He held the radio to his lips. "All right, go ahead."

The radio squawked; then we heard Lynette's voice. "Mom, I'm here! I'm all right. Can you hear me?"

"Honey! Where are you? What happened?"

The line crackled, and Lynette's voice went in and out. The basic story was that she and Bryce had gotten lost during the storm. They were inside a cabin, and both were fine.

Finally Bryce came on the walkie-talkie. "Ash? You'll never believe who we found. Vanessa. She's all right."

People crowded around us, and Marion hugged me. "I just knew he'd be okay."

I called Mom and she was as relieved as I was.

The security guy said they'd fire up the snowmobiles after sunup.

I fell into bed praying, thanking God.

# CHAPTER 62

☻ *Bryce* ☻

*After Lynette talked to her mother,* she and Vanessa danced around the cabin until they got cold and retreated to the fire. I was glad we'd reached someone, but I couldn't figure out how the radio had gotten under the bed. Vanessa said she hadn't seen it before.

I sliced more SPAM for breakfast, but the girls said they weren't hungry. We drank the water bottles I'd found and watched the darkened window, waiting for the sun. The wind howled and pattered wet snow against it.

"You think they'll be able to get here with those snowmobiles?" Vanessa said.

"That's the only way they'll get here," I said.

"What about the guy who brought you here?" Lynette said. "Think he'll come back?"

"He probably saw you guys coming and took off," Vanessa said. "Best thing that could've happened to me."

"So you haven't seen anyone, right?" I said.

"I kept waking up and drinking that tainted water. I don't remember anything."

They sat on the mattress and covered up.

"What do you compete in?" Vanessa said to me.

I told her and Lynette said, "You should see his routine. It's really funny."

"You've seen me perform?"

"I watched a video someone made of you. It's good."

"Do it," Vanessa said.

"Now? Here?"

"It'll be perfect practice for the second round," Lynette said.

"Yeah, but—"

"I won't take no for an answer," Vanessa said. "Do it or we'll throw SPAM at you."

# CHAPTER 63

❀ Ashley ❀

Mrs. Jarvis woke me, and we watched the snowmobiles move out. It was light outside, but the snow was still coming down sideways. The security guys had called the police and assured them they'd handle the rescue.

"The police want to talk to Vanessa when she gets back," one security guard said.

We watched the two machines motor over the new-fallen snow until they became specks against the ski slope and disappeared. The whining motors drifted and eventually faded into the whistling wind.

As everyone went to breakfast, some kids yelled and laughed, excited to go tubing or sledding.

I was fiddling with the cereal dispenser, trying to figure out how it worked, when Mrs. Jarvis came up to me. Raisin Bran spilled on the floor.

"I need to talk to you," she said.

I wet a napkin and tried to clean the mess. "Yeah, sure."

I followed her to a table. She cradled a cup of coffee like it was an only child. "I want to tell you I'm sorry for jumping to conclusions and for accusing you and your brother." She took a sip, and I moved a couple of raisins around in my plastic bowl. "From what Lynette told me on the radio, your brother was a big help."

"Did Lynette say why Vanessa was there?"

"Something about being kidnapped. Lynette said the water in the cabin had been spiked."

"Some kind of drug?"

She nodded. "I guess they won't know until the police investigate." She blew into the hot liquid. "Who would want to do a thing like that?"

**CHAPTER 64**

☺ *Bryce* ☺

*Vanessa and Lynette laughed at my routine.*

Vanessa said I was good. "You'll be a hit in high school plays, because there aren't as many boys going out for parts."

Ashley talks about high school and even college, but I can't. Just seems so far away.

We got a call on the radio from one of the security guards, asking about our cabin's location. I walked outside and told him what I saw from there.

We grabbed our stuff and walked out the front door. In the distance came a buzzing, snarling sound. It was either a bear with a sinus infection or a snowmobile.

Vanessa and Lynette whooped when they saw the two machines. We ran to them, waving and yelling.

The first guard pulled up, got off, and checked us for injuries. When he was satisfied that we were okay, he looked at me. "We can only take two now. You mind staying for our second run?"

"Just make sure you come back."

He gave the girls water bottles and made them drink. He threw one to me, then tossed a brown paper bag. "Have some of this while we're gone," he yelled, starting up his machine. "It'll keep you from starving."

The shape of the bag felt familiar, and I groaned. A can of SPAM.

I hurried back to the cabin and returned the bedding. I put the last logs on the fire and sat close. I felt a sudden gust of wind and turned around.

The door was open, and a mountain of a man stared at me.

## CHAPTER 65

❦ Ashley ❦

The snowmobiles' return was like watching astronauts land. People cheered, waved, and clapped. Two local TV stations had trucks on the scene with cameras going, panning faces in the crowd. I asked a guy in the passenger side of one of the trucks how he'd gotten through the closed roads.

"We can go wherever we want," he said. He was young, had a mustache, and wore a sweater and a tie under his coat. "This is a real human-interest story."

"How'd you find out about it?" I said.

He shrugged. "A call came in to the assignment editor. She checked it with the police."

"A call from who?"

"Someone at the school. Listen, kid, I got work to do, okay?"

"Wait. Do you have a card?" I flashed him my brightest I'm-a-cute-little-girl-and-I-want-to-be-on-TV-someday smile.

He rolled his eyes and handed me one. It had the station logo on it in red, white, and green; his name; and a phone number.

"What's the name of your assignment editor?" I said.

"Kathy White," he yelled over his shoulder.

The man's camera operator shot the snowmobiles making their triumphal entry. Bryce wasn't with them.

Both stations got a shot of Lynette and her mother embracing. Several people greeted Vanessa, including Jen. I broke away from them and went back to the dorm to find a phone.

The line rang twice before a woman answered. She sounded stressed, like she was trying to do 10 things at once. "News desk."

"Hi, I'm looking for Kathy White."

"Got her."

"Yeah, I'm here at CSD where they just found—"

"The news truck there?" she interrupted.

"Yeah, and I saw your reporter too."

"Good, they made it. Now what—?" The phone rang. "Hang on a second."

"Sure."

There was some weird music on the line, and about a minute later she came back. "Okay, what's up?"

"I heard you got a tip about the missing people."

"People? I only heard something about an actress. Vanessa something."

"Two kids found her. Who told you about Vanessa?"

"I talked with him myself—he didn't want to be identified."

"Why not?"

"How am I supposed to know? He just gave me the information and said it would be big news." The phone rang, and she sighed. "Gotta go."

"Wait! Do you know where the guy was calling from?"

"Yeah, the caller ID said it was something called Harris Hall."

I wanted to thank her for the information, but some people don't give you the chance.

# CHAPTER 66

◑ *Bryce* ◑

*The man was over six feet tall.* Maybe 300 pounds. It was hard to tell because he had on a coat as big as a grizzly bear. His beard was dark, and he had a nose the size of a cucumber. Reminded me of Hagrid in those Harry Potter movies. It was the same face I'd seen in the window—a guy big enough to carry a girl to this cabin.

He just looked at me and I stared back. He turned to leave without saying anything, and I couldn't keep quiet. "What are you doing out here?"

He glanced back and raised a massive eyebrow. "What am *I* doing out here?" His voice was as deep as a bass drum. "The question is, what are *you* doing here? I thought you'd left."

"They're coming back for me after they take the girls."

"What I thought," he said, smiling, showing scraggly teeth. "You're the chivalrous one."

"Excuse me?"

He waved a hand. "I live on the other side of the mountain. I saw a light last night in the storm, figured someone was stuck, so I came to help."

*Likely story,* I thought. "So it wasn't you with the light?"

"I had one, but I didn't flash it all around like a monkey in a tree." He imitated the flashlight's beam dancing in the wind. "I saw you and a girl stumbling around. I figured you'd find the cabin, especially with that guy waving his light, drawing you."

"Wait, you think someone was luring us here?" I said.

"Yeah, I saw him. After you went inside, he climbed down the mountain. If you know the way, you can get right to the school from here."

My mind swirled. "What did he look like?"

"Couldn't see his face, but he was wiry. Looked like a student. I've seen him up here from time to time. Wore a dark coat." He walked to the ridge and lifted a massive hand. "Good luck!"

The man's voice echoed through the woods and was replaced by the hum of a snowmobile's motor. When I looked back at the ridge, he was gone.

PART 3

**CHAPTER 67**

❃ Ashley ❃

Vanessa came to her room and put her stuff in a suitcase. She said she would room with Rhonda, the girl at the dress shop, until we left. She didn't talk a lot to me and I wanted to ask a bunch of questions, but she left so fast that I couldn't.

Bryce finally came down the mountain at 8:30, and the news trucks were gone. After I hugged him, he said, "I have to talk with you."

"Make it quick—my round is in a half hour."

He told me what Mountain Man had said and what had happened in the cabin overnight. "There's something weird going on, Ash, and I can't put it together."

I told him what I'd discovered about Vanessa while he was gone.

He scratched his chin. "Go to your competition. I'm gonna take a shower and get to mine. Let's meet for lunch."

"Got it." I ran toward the drama building.

Marion met me at the door. "I wish I could stay to watch, but my second round starts at nine too."

I wished her well, as if she needed it, and walked into the room a few minutes before nine.

Everyone looked up and stared. The room was packed. I sat in the first chair I could find and saw my name in the first position on the blackboard. Not even time to catch my breath.

The judges welcomed us and gave the rules for spectators.

Then it was my turn. I took a deep breath and walked to the front.

# CHAPTER 68

☽ *Bryce* ☽

**I felt a lot better** after I'd showered and gotten dressed. I went to the dining hall, but all the food was gone. I thought about going into town for something—anything to get the SPAM taste out of my mouth—but there wasn't enough time.

I jumped in the elevator and made it to my room. I had just enough time to grab my script and make it across the courtyard, but I couldn't find the script. I knew I had put it on the desk in the room, but it wasn't there. I checked in my overnight bag, the living room, even the bathroom. Kael and Mr. Gminski were gone.

In a final act of desperation I looked through the trash. It wasn't there. I sat on the bed, thinking. The loss of sleep through the night had me on edge, and tears sprung to my eyes.

Then it hit me. I knew my routine inside out. I could do it in my sleep. All I needed was something that looked like my script. Mr. Gminski had sample scripts on his desk, and I grabbed one and looked at the clock. I had five minutes.

I ran downstairs, hit the fire door, and faced a courtyard filled with snow. I found a path the grounds crew had made and slipped and slid to the building. I was out of breath and my feet were dripping wet when I reached the front desk. They told me my competition was on the third floor.

Everyone looked up at me as I wheezed and found a chair. I was catching my breath when the first competitor stood and took her place. I glanced at the lineup on the board, glad I wasn't first. My name wasn't there.

She began, and I recognized the routine—"The Highwayman." *This is Oral Interp of Poetry,* I thought. I was in the wrong room.

I said a bad word in my head and kept saying it over and over. I couldn't just get up and leave, but if I sat here, I'd miss my competition.

I stood and walked straight out the door. I didn't look back to see if the judges stopped the girl, but I hoped it didn't throw her off. I found the right room and slipped in. They had waited for me, but my time was almost up.

"Mr. Timberline, it's good to see you," a judge said from the back.

I was fifth on the list, which gave me time to calm down. When I stood, I felt the fatigue in my bones, tasted the SPAM and my sour stomach, and saw Mountain Man every time I closed my eyes. But when I took my place at the front, I tried to think of how much Mom and Sam would root for me.

When you do a routine over and over, it can become stale. The humor fades, and you forget that some people have never heard it. But something came over me—a renewed energy or a freedom I hadn't felt before—and I performed my routine like it was the first time. The audience got into it. The judges laughed. By the time I was done, I knew nobody could touch that performance.

I sat and watched the last competitor. The guy was good but not as good as me.

Right after we finished, a kid came walking in with a piece of paper and handed it to a judge. We all got up to leave, but one of the judges called my name and asked me to step to the back. I thought she was going to compliment me on my performance or say that I had the highest score. Instead, she asked to see my script.

*Gulp.*

"I couldn't find my script this morning," I said, handing the pages to her. "I grabbed this instead."

"You know you're supposed to have a copy of the script you perform," she said. "If you don't, you're disqualified."

My mind spun. My cell phone ringing in the first round. My script missing this morning. They weren't accidents.

"Why did you ask me for my script and not the others?" I said.

The judge didn't answer. She just made a few notes on the evaluation sheet.

I wanted to tell her this was a setup. I wanted to defend myself or explain that I'd been trapped in a cabin all night. Instead, I took Mr. Gminski's script and walked out.

# CHAPTER 69

✹ Ashley ✹

I ran from the building and dodged people in the narrow snow path. I wanted to make it back to my room before I exploded.

"Ashley, wait!" Marion called. She ran to me, and I hid my eyes. "How'd you do?" she said.

"I just want to go back to my room."

"That bad, huh?"

"Awful. I've never frozen like that. I couldn't remember a couple of lines, and it messed the whole thing up."

"It's okay. It's just a dumb old tournament."

When we got in the elevator I asked how she did.

"Okay, I guess."

"You didn't get an alien question again, did you?"

She smiled.

When we got off the elevator, Jen was there. "Tough day?" she said.

I nodded.

"Come to my room. I'm an expert at bad days." She led us inside and got two natural sodas from a small refrigerator. It made me want to go to college just so I could have one.

"I heard your brother made it back," Jen said. "Must have been kind of scary."

I wondered if Jen was trying to get information. Had she been part of Vanessa's kidnapping?

I told her about Bryce—nothing specific, just that he was cold and tired when he returned and that everyone was okay. Then I sneezed and looked for a tissue.

"In the bathroom," Jen said.

I blew my nose with toilet paper and looked in the mirror at my red eyes and nose. It would have been funny if it hadn't been so tragic. My trip to Hollywood, my future, my life—they had all ended with one performance.

I was about to leave when I spotted something on top of the medicine cabinet. It was a brown bottle, a liquid of some sort. I didn't recognize the name, but the label said *induces sleep.*

Could this be what they had used to spike Vanessa's water? I wondered.

"You okay in there?" Jen said.

"Yeah, be right out."

☺ *Bryce* ☺

*After the competition* I went back to my room and fell into bed without changing. I slept and dreamed about Mountain Man. He chased me down the ski slope until an avalanche covered us. Somehow there was an air pocket, and we wound up in kind of an igloo. He pulled out Rook cards and we played a few hands. Weird.

I opened my eyes, wondering what it meant, and I saw Mr. Gminski at my door holding something. "I heard what happened," he said.

"I wasn't trying to cheat. I couldn't find—"

He held up my script, covered with coffee stains and what looked like jelly.

"Where'd you find it?"

"Trash can in the dining hall. A worker noticed it. You didn't throw it away?"

"I left it right here in my room." I rubbed my eyes and sat up.

"I'm going to talk to the judges," Mr. Gminski said. "I think they'll understand when they hear—"

"No, don't do that." It had all come together in my mind. I knew who had sabotaged me.

"Bryce, you had the highest score in that round. You'd be in the finals if they hadn't disqualified you."

"I know. But I think this might be more important."

## CHAPTER 71

❀ Ashley ❀

After Marion and I left Jen's room, I couldn't get the bottle out of my mind. I phoned security and told them what I'd seen.

"You really think Jen's involved?" Marion said when I hung up.

"It looks strange to me," I said.

We went to our room and sat in front of the TV. Marion flipped through the channels and found a newscast. Lynette sat with her mom and looked as upset as I was.

"Did your second round go as badly as mine?" I said.

"It was okay," Lynette said. "Kael and I got second place."

"That's great. So what's wrong?"

She shook her head and ran to her room, her mom not far behind.

"Take a look at this," Marion said, turning up the sound.

It was the reporter I had met standing near the entrance to CSD. ". . . discovered in a remote cabin by two students attending a speech competition. The girl is fine now, after being drugged and held in the cabin, but she says she regrets missing the chance of a lifetime to audition for a Hollywood movie."

They cut to Vanessa, her face framed next to a blazing fireplace. "I don't know what I'd have done if Lynn and Brent hadn't found me up there," she said, a tear dropping onto her cheek.

"Did she say Brent?" Marion said.

"I'd been practicing my whole life for a chance like that, and now it's gone," Vanessa said, her chin quivering.

Marion flipped through the channels until we heard a commotion in the hallway.

A security officer stood outside Jen's door. "Do you have anything like that in your room?" he said.

"I don't even have any prescriptions," Jen said. "Just some Tylenol and aspirin."

"Would you mind if we looked?" the officer said.

"Sure, go ahead."

The officer went inside. I felt bad for Jen because I was the one who had tipped them off.

"They think I had something to do with Vanessa's disappearance," she whispered. "Why would they think that?"

The officer came back with the bottle in a plastic bag. "Recognize this?"

Jen stared at it. "I've never seen it before. You found this in my room?"

"We haven't done tests yet, but this drug is used to knock people out."

Jen looked shocked. It was either a really good act or someone had planted that bottle.

# CHAPTER 72

☻ *Bryce* ☻

*I found Kael eating alone* in the dining area. He seemed surprised to see me. "You look good for having lived through a blizzard."

"Looks like your ankle is a lot better too," I said.

I asked about his performance and he told me. He didn't ask what had happened at my performance.

"How's it going with Lynette?" I said.

"Okay, I guess. She said you really kept your wits about you up on the mountain."

I nodded, just looking at him as I ate.

"What?"

I smiled, wiped my hands on a napkin, then drained my soda. I watched Kael out of the corner of my eye. I'd been his friend long enough to know that he was getting nervous. I decided to put it all on the table. "I know what happened."

He looked at me, startled. "What?"

"Lynette had you turn my cell phone on. You gave her my number."

"What are you talking about?"

"And when you hurt your ankle, which is kind of hard to do with the boots you were wearing, she led me back to the ski slope and acted nice. That way you could get my script."

"Bryce, you're crazy! You think I'd—"

"You and Mr. Gminski are the only ones with a key to our room."

He couldn't think of anything to say.

"Look, you probably thought she was just playing a prank," I said. "You didn't know she would go this far."

"I wanted to give the script back—honest. I saw her write a note to the judges and couldn't believe she was ratting on you. She left after we finished our competition, and I saw her give the paper to some kid in the hallway."

"I've known she hasn't liked me, but I never thought she could be this mean." I looked at him. "And I didn't think you'd do something like this."

"I'm sorry, man. It really got out of hand. You deserve to go to the finals."

"Well, I'm not."

"You want me to talk to the judges?"

I shook my head.

"What are you going to do?"

"Talk to Lynette."

# CHAPTER 73

❀ Ashley ❀

The whole campus was abuzz with the news about Jen, but everyone knew she couldn't have been working alone. It would make sense if her boyfriend, Hunter, had helped.

I found Bryce at lunch. He looked like someone had stolen his ATV. I asked what was wrong.

He frowned. "Lots. What's up?"

I told him what had happened to Jen and asked about Hunter.

"Let's go see him," Bryce said.

When we got to Hunter's room, the security guards were standing in the hallway with Jen and asking Hunter questions. Bryce and I slipped around the corner.

"Tuesday night I was over at Top Billing shooting pool," Hunter said.

"Anybody see you?"

"Yeah, all the guys I played with."

"What time did you leave?"

"We stayed till it closed at 11, then went over to a friend's house."

"When did you leave there?"

"I actually stayed the whole night." Hunter looked at Jen and pursed his lips. "But, Jen . . . I have to tell them."

"Tell them what?" she said.

"Jen asked if I had anything that would help her sleep. My mom had a prescription, and I gave it to her."

"What? Hunter, you know that—"

"I never thought she'd use it on someone else. . . ."

"Hunter!" Jen yelled.

The guards separated them. Jen continued to say she had never seen the medicine bottle.

Bryce and I talked in the lounge. He told me about the situation with Lynette, and I couldn't believe she had sabotaged his performances. "What are you going to do?"

"I keep asking myself what Jesus would do," he said. "Part of me wants to forgive her, and the other part wants to push her off a building."

"You should tell Mr. Gminski," I said.

"I'll let you know what I decide."

The security guards left Jen alone. She sat on the arm of an overstuffed chair and cried. "I thought he loved me," she said. "He's selling me out."

"Why would Hunter do that?"

She shook her head. It could have all been an act, but her shock looked genuine. "I never asked him for any medicine. And he never gave me any. Plus, how am I supposed to overpower Vanessa and drag her someplace I've never seen?"

I put a hand on her shoulder and looked into her eyes, trying to see if she was telling the truth.

# CHAPTER 74

☺ *Bryce* ☺

*The finals would be held* in two auditoriums. Kael, Lynette, and Marion made it. Ashley and I didn't. We would be spectators instead of participants.

I retreated to my room, trying to figure out what to do about Lynette. I didn't want to call Mom and whine like some little kid, and I couldn't go to Mr. Gminski. I wished I could talk with my real dad. He would have a good answer. That's when I thought of Sam. Even though he's not a Christian, he's had wise advice in the past.

"Sounds like they're in a pickle," Sam said after I'd explained everything. "You could nail them if you wanted."

"Yeah. I'm just not sure I want to."

Sam waited a long time. "This is the same girl who caused all the trouble with Jeff's climbing wall, isn't it?"

"Yeah."

"Well, you could tell your teacher and let him handle it. Write Kael off your friend list and avoid them both."

"Doesn't sound like you think that's what I should do."

"Bryce, I don't go to church much—you know that. But the last time I was there, the pastor talked about Christians being forgiven and showing that forgiveness to others."

"I remember." It hadn't been the usual turn-your-cheek-and-let-people-slap-you-around kind of sermon. The pastor made the point that Christians were to take the lead in forgiving.

"The way I look at it," Sam continued, "what they did to you was wrong and deserves to be punished. They spilled a pitcher of milk on your performance. You have every right to cry foul and get justice. But loving them may mean that you absorb that wrong, like a sponge picking up the milk. They should apologize and own up to it, of course."

"I like the sponge thing. Thanks, Sam."

# CHAPTER 75

❀ Ashley ❀

We were all invited to a banquet Friday night. The storm had let up late in the day, and forecasters said the worst was over. Word spread that Jen had been taken to the police station. Also, some producers of a Denver talk show wanted Vanessa as a guest. Someone said Oprah Winfrey's producer had called, but I thought that might be a rumor.

The main dining hall was laid out with nice silverware and plates and candles at each table. We were supposed to sit with our team, but Marion was the only one we could find. (Bryce scowled.)

Professor Hopper of the drama department was our host. He said a lot of funny stuff about speech tournaments, and everybody laughed, especially the people who were in the finals.

Some students, including Wendell, were our waiters and waitresses. They brought food and filled our water glasses.

Every time someone opened the front door, a blast of cold air blew through the room. At one point, I saw a guy run in and hang up his coat, then head to the kitchen.

"Wasn't that Hunter?" Bryce said.

"I think so."

Bryce got a weird look on his face. "When he comes out, keep him busy."

"What are you going to do?"

"Just keep him busy," he said.

Bryce waited at the back of the hall. Soon Hunter came out of the kitchen holding a tray of desserts. It was some kind of chocolate thing that tasted so good I could have eaten the whole tray. Another guy served us. When Hunter's tray was almost empty, I looked for Bryce. He was gone.

I stood and blocked Hunter from the kitchen. "I didn't know you'd be serving," I said.

He stopped, a puzzled look on his face.

"I'm Bryce's sister. He's on your floor?"

"Oh yeah, Bryce. Good kid. You his twin?"

I nodded. "But I'm older by 57 seconds."

He laughed, lowering the tray and putting it under his arm. "Well, I should keep moving—there's a lot of desserts to serve."

"Yeah, I was just wondering, is there anything other than chocolate?"

"Some people are allergic to it," he said. "We have an alternative—it's pecan pie. Can I get you one of those?"

"That would be great," I said. He was about to hurry off, and I still didn't see Bryce. "Oh, could you take mine away? I don't even want to be tempted by it."

"Sure," he said.

I led Hunter the long way to my table, gave him Bryce's untouched pie, and thanked him.

Finally Bryce returned. "What happened to my dessert?" he said when he sat down.

"You're allergic. You get pecan."

"I hate pecan."

"It was the only way I could occupy Hunter. What did you do back there?"

"Got some clues. I think I might have this one solved, but I need your help."

# CHAPTER 76

○ *Bryce* ○

*I walked quickly back to the dorm* and changed. There's something about nice clothes that make me itch all over, and I couldn't wait to get out of them.

After I changed, I looked for Kael but he wasn't there. I stopped on the girls' floor and asked around, but no one had seen him or Lynette. I waited in the lobby, watching the front door. I figured they'd gone to eat by themselves.

Wendell was at the desk, and I asked if he had kept up with the situation with Jen.

"Yeah, she's the last girl I would have picked to be a kidnapper. Guess she had motive though."

"I still have my doubts about her."

"Really? Who do you think did it?"

I wasn't about to tell him my theory, but I did need his help. "Custodians have a master key, right?"

He jingled the ring attached to his pocket. "I can get in just about any building around here."

"How about the main auditorium and the sound room?"

"Sure."

"Well, I think we can catch the culprit tomorrow night if you can help."

His eyes grew wide, and I figured he was thinking of a story. This whole thing could become a script for one of his classes. "What time tomorrow?"

It was after 10 when Kael and Lynette walked inside with Lynette's mother. They had food in Styrofoam containers, and Lynette's mother took them to a large refrigerator in the commons area.

"Mind if I have a word with you two?" I said, stepping out of the shadows.

Lynette almost jumped when she saw me. Kael looked at the floor. It's funny how interesting the floor gets when you're guilty.

"My mom will be back—"

"This won't take long," I said.

She moved into the dark and stood across from me. I could see her face silhouetted by the light from the front desk. She was pretty, and I wished there was some way I could tell her that. Not now, of course.

"Before you start," she said, "Kael told me that you know."

"The whole thing at the cabin, treating me nicely—that was a good act," I said.

"I don't know what I was thinking. I mean, I've been mad at you since I first met you. You made fun of me in class and brought up all that Christian stuff."

I didn't remember making fun of her, but I didn't want to interrupt.

"I thought for a long time about how I could get back at you, get even. Put you in your place. That's when I came up with this. It seemed perfect, and I thought you'd never figure—"

"Lynette?" Mrs. Jarvis said. She moved past the elevators and found us in the dark. "Are you coming, dear?"

"In a minute, Mom," she said.

"All right, but you've got a big day tomorrow." She got in the elevator, and the doors closed.

"I guess I'm trying to make an excuse for what I did. And there is no excuse. I take full responsibility for it—it wasn't Kael's fault. And I deserve whatever Mr. Gminski decides."

There it was. The milk was on the floor. I could splash around in it, throw it back on them, or drop the sponge. *God's sponge,* I thought. *Kind of has a ring to it.*

"Mr. Gminski doesn't have to know," I said.

"Why not?"

"Because I forgive you. It's over. Forgotten. Well, not forgotten, because it's kind of hard to forget losing a chance to go to Hollywood...." I smiled. "You don't have to worry about me making you pay." I turned to Kael. "You okay with that?"

"Yeah, how could I not be?"

"Wait," Lynette said, shaking her head. "That's it? You're not going to rat us out to Mr. Gminski or try to get us back during the finals?"

"Lynette, I like you. I hope you guys win. It really hurt that you treated me that way, but I've done stupid things before. Probably will again, and I hope somebody will forgive me. So you're both off the hook. Break a leg." I patted Kael on the shoulder and walked away.

As fast as my heart was beating, I felt good. God's sponge did the trick.

# CHAPTER 77

✖ Ashley ✖

You could feel the excitement in the air at the finals. Bryce and I sat together and watched the Oral Interp of Humor competition. The girl who won was excellent, and Bryce admitted that even his best performance might not have been enough to beat her.

It was painful to watch Kael and Lynette because I knew too much. They were shaking when the routine began, then settled in and only muffed a line or two, but that was enough to give them fourth place.

Marion's Impromptu competition was after lunch, and just watching made me sweat. It's one thing to speak in front of a roomful of spectators. It's another to speak to an audience of hundreds, ready to judge every word.

The first contestant chose a subject related to teenage drinking. His point was that if 18-year-olds could go to war and fight for their country, they ought to legally be able to drink alcohol. I've read too many stories about drunk drivers killing people, so I didn't agree, but he made his points.

Marion was the next-to-last contestant. She walked onstage, looked over the note cards on a little table, pushed one aside, and held up the other two. I was dying to see her topics. My palms were sweaty as a red light flashed.

"Miss Quidley, your subject?" a judge said.

Marion picked a topic, and the judge started a timer. We all watched the red hand tick down.

Marion sat, flicking the card with an index finger and staring at it. She jotted a few words on a card, scratched them out, and started again. The red hand passed a minute, and I looked at Bryce. He'd never seen Marion in competition before.

Finally Marion looked at the clock, took a deep breath, and walked to the microphone.

# CHAPTER 78

☻ *Bryce* ☻

*As Marion gathered her thoughts,* kids whispered and rattled programs. Marion blocked the noise out, like a NASCAR driver with cars around him going 200 mph. She was totally focused.

The room fell deathly quiet when she started. "My topic is the importance of the separation between church and state. The founding fathers of our country knew from experience that a government-sponsored, government-imposed religious system was oppressive. It didn't make people follow a higher power—it made them resent the intrusion into their lives. So these founding fathers, in their documents and writings, made sure that the government stayed out of religion, didn't impose a set of beliefs, and left it up to the people to choose whether to be Christian, Muslim, Buddhist, Hindu, or no religion at all.

"But it's clear from their writings that this wall of separation was intended to protect the people from government intrusion, not the other way around. Our freedom of speech—our right to be heard on matters we think are important—is built into the fabric of our founding documents. So what happens when we want to speak up about a religious matter?"

Marion's voice was clear, and she used the microphone well. Instead of looking down or away, she looked directly at the audience. The room remained quiet. Every eye was focused on Marion Quidley.

"In our school in Red Rock, we had a classmate named Jeff Alexander. Jeff was funny and smart, and he also happened to be an outspoken Christian. He didn't shove it down people's throats, but when a subject came up that had something to do with his spiritual beliefs, he gave his opinion. Some students thought he was too religious, while others applauded. I don't think Jeff cared what others thought.

"Jeff was unique because he didn't just talk about his faith; he lived it. When he got cancer, he prayed to be healed. When his condition worsened, he made plans for the afterlife and for the present. He asked a group to give him a last wish—to build a climbing wall for the kids of Red Rock. He asked that a Bible verse be framed at the top of that climbing wall. The people gave him his wish, but Jeff was never able to see the wall. He died shortly before it was unveiled.

"This fall, a student objected to that plaque, contending that her rights were violated. This was government sponsorship of religion, she said. This violated the separation of church and state. School officials took down the verse, and now Jeff's parents have the plaque in their garage.

"I do believe separation of church and state is important, but not to keep kids from hearing religious speech. Separation of church and state should continue because the voices of people like Jeff Alexander should not be silenced."

# CHAPTER 79

❋ Ashley ❋

I couldn't believe what I was hearing. I knew Marion didn't have to believe what she was saying, but it seemed like she had owned every syllable. She paused and looked at the time. There were two minutes left.

Marion cleared her throat and flexed her hands, then finally began again. "Speaking personally, I've been an agnostic—a person who is open to new information but doesn't believe there's enough evidence to prove God does or doesn't exist. But that's changed. I was excited when I learned I'd get to compete here. Then my joy turned to regret because my family doesn't have much money. We couldn't afford the fee, and Mom said I couldn't come.

"I tried doing odd jobs, and my mom asked if she could get an advance on her salary, but nothing worked. That's when I prayed. For the first time I asked God—if he existed—to work it out so I could go. And then I made a bargain. I told him that if he would do this, I'd find some way to tell people about it and that I would learn about him. Follow him.

"I never thought it would happen. And when my coach said someone had donated the money and I could go, I'd forgotten all about the prayer." Her voice caught with emotion, and she paused.

For the rest of the speech, her chin quivered, and she looked straight at me. "So, in order to keep my promise, I was going to tell a friend about it this weekend. She's a Christian and she really believes the whole God thing, and I can tell it's changed her life. And I want that kind of life too. But I guess I've told all of you, and that makes my point. If we silence talk of God in school and in government, and we say you should keep that separate—you should only do that on weekends or at home—then we don't have freedom of speech. We have a government-imposed silence on a topic.

"I believe in the separation of church and state in the sense that the government shouldn't impose its will on our beliefs. But people of faith should not be kept from contributing, speaking, running for office, or having a voice in schools. That would weaken both church and state, and we would all be poorer for it."

The clock dinged. The five minutes were up.

Marion walked from the microphone, and I began the applause. I stood, tears in my eyes. I had prayed for Marion a long time. I had spoken to her about God. I hadn't even known she was listening.

After the competition, I went up to her.

She hugged me and smiled. "I don't suppose Lynette or her mother liked that speech very much."

"Bryce said he thought it was the best he'd heard."

"Really?"

I nodded. "Did you really mean all that? You said that you didn't have to believe the stuff you talked about."

"I couldn't have made all that up."

I laughed. "We need to talk about your theology. What if God hadn't answered your prayer? What if you didn't get the money to go?"

She looked at the note card in her hand. "He's been trying to get my attention for a long time. I have a feeling that if he didn't answer this one, it would have happened down the road."

Marion looked behind me and I turned.

It was Lynette. She reached out a hand and shook Marion's. "Good job," she said.

# CHAPTER 80

◎ *Bryce* ◎

*As good as I thought Marion's speech was,* the judges gave her second place behind a guy whose topic was steroid use in high school athletics.

Mr. Gminski was pleased. No other team had two entries in the finals. He took us all to dinner later in the afternoon, but it was hard to eat when I had so much on my mind.

While the others settled into the lounge downstairs and watched a movie, Ashley and I put our plan into action. We did surveillance on the suspects, checking as much as we could to make sure we knew where each was.

Ashley pulled out the card that Eleanor, the woman with the famous director, had given her, and wrote a note on the back: *Meet me at 10 in the drama building. Side door will be open. Don't tell anyone.*

I wrote the same note, only I put it on some stationery Ashley had found in Vanessa's room.

At 9:00 we separated. I went upstairs to the dorm, located the right room, and shoved the note under the door. I left a little bit of it sticking out and moved across the hall. There was loud music coming from inside.

At 9:30, when the paper hadn't moved, I went to the door, jiggled the knob, and ran for the stairs.

Nothing. The music still blared.

I dialed the phone and hung up.

The music suddenly stopped, and I tiptoed to the door, jiggled the knob again, and raced for the stairs.

This time the door opened. Seconds later it closed, and the piece of paper disappeared.

*Bingo!*

# CHAPTER 81

❀ Ashley ❀

Bryce and I were in our places by 9:45. Wendell had opened the side door for us and stayed with me in the recording room at the back. In the whole auditorium there was only one tiny bulb burning above the stage.

Bryce had taken his place in the balcony. He was hunkered down below the railing, wearing a pair of wireless headphones.

I found out that Wendell hadn't started out as a writer but in technical direction. He spent some time running sound and showed me how to turn on the stage microphone and how to record. Bryce would listen to what we were hearing, and I could speak to him through a Talk-back button.

A little before 10, Vanessa walked onstage dressed to kill. She had on a silky dress, and her hair was perfect. I guess she thought Eleanor had actually given her the message.

"Hello?" Vanessa said. "Anybody here?"

We could hear her through the booth monitors, but the auditorium speakers were off.

She walked across the stage, looking into the rows of seats. "Eleanor? It's me, Vanessa."

After a few trips back and forth, she sat on the edge and let her legs dangle, swinging them like a child. She checked her watch, holding it up to the light so she could see.

When the side door opened, she jumped up, primped her hair, and straightened her outfit.

Hunter walked in from the shadows.

Vanessa put her hands on her hips. "You? I thought Eleanor was going to be here."

"You're not excited to see me, huh?" He walked across the stage and hugged her. Then kissed her. "You doing okay?"

She pushed him away and whispered, "We don't know who's here. Did you put this under my door?"

He looked at the card. "No. I've never seen it before. Did you write this note?"

She took the note and read it quickly. "No." Then she lowered her voice even more. "Hunter, someone knows."

He grabbed her shoulders and held her an arm's length away. "No, they don't. No one suspects anything. They still have Jen at the police station. They found the drug in her bathroom where I put it." He looked into her eyes. "You're going to have that audition. You'll go on *Oprah*, and you'll get so much exposure that the producers will be knocking down your door."

He kissed her on the forehead and hugged her. That's when the spotlight hit them.

"Who's up there?" Hunter said.

"Hello?" Vanessa said.

The two held their hands in front of their faces, blocking the light as Bryce began to clap.

"Who is it?" Vanessa whispered. "Do you think they heard us?"

"Not from up there. No way."

Bryce stood and Vanessa spotted him. "Bruce? Is that you?"

"It's Bryce."

"Right."

"Did you write these notes?" Hunter said. There was an edge to his voice.

"Just found something in your coat," Bryce said. "Thought you'd want it back."

Hunter shoved his hands in the pockets of his dark blue coat.

"What's he talking about?" Vanessa said.

"The letter you wrote me when you were at the cabin," Hunter said. "I had it in my pocket."

Bryce waved something in front of the light. "'I can't wait to get back to you, Snookey,'" he called. "Is that what you call him, Vanessa?"

I was glad I was in a soundproof booth because I was laughing so hard.

Hunter jumped from the stage and ran along the front row, looking into the balcony.

"Careful, Bruce," I said over the talk back, but Bryce had taken his headphones off. He dropped the pages, and they floated down to Hunter.

"These are photocopies!" Hunter yelled.

"Yeah, I don't have the originals, if that's what you're looking for."

Hunter stopped. "Where are they?"

"Not sure, but the security guards said something about taking them to the police station. I guess one of the guards is good friends with Jen. And another one told me there are two radios missing from the security locker. Any idea where those are?"

Hunter climbed onto the stage.

"The same guard said you used to work in security before you became an RA," Bryce continued. "Is that right?"

"Come on," Hunter growled at Vanessa.

That's when I hit the playback and Wendell turned on the stage speakers. The recording hissed a little, but you could clearly hear Vanessa say, "Hunter, someone knows."

"No, they don't. No one suspects anything. They still have Jen at the police station. They found the drug in her bathroom where I put it."

I stopped the recording. Vanessa and Hunter were as frozen as snowmen, not knowing which way to turn. Finally Hunter jumped down and ran toward Wendell and me.

We turned on the lights inside the recording room and locked the door. Wendell pointed at the digital recorder, then wagged his finger at Hunter, which I thought was funny.

Vanessa ran out the side door, and a blast of air blew the curtains around on the stage. I heard a siren.

Hunter ran to the doors behind us, but they were all locked. He turned, flew down the aisle, leaped onto the stage, and followed Vanessa.

# CHAPTER 82

◯ *Bryce* ◯

*It was a perfect performance* by Ashley and Wendell. I clapped for them as they made a CD and a backup recording of Hunter and Vanessa's conversation.

Vanessa ran into Phil, the elk, and he cornered her against the science building until the security guys heard her screaming and rescued her.

The police found Hunter hiding in the Harris Hall stairwell. He told them the whole scheme had been Vanessa's idea, planned a month before the audition. She figured the extra publicity of her being taken to a remote cabin would be good for her career. The storm just made the story better. Once she returned, she would become famous through interviews, and producers would clamor for her.

Hunter wanted me to find Vanessa; that's why he tried to lure me into the backwoods. I didn't bite, so he went back to the cabin but got turned around himself. When he saw Lynette and me, he waved his light, trying to get us to come in his direction. After we made it, he found the shortcut back to the school.

Jen was cleared of any wrongdoing, which pleased Ashley.

I was glad that we'd solved the mystery, but I still had some bad feelings about Kael and Lynette. Even though I'd said I'd forgiven them, I still felt hurt. Like any deep wound, I guess it'll take some time to heal.

Then we found out that Mr. Gminski had been offered a job by CSD. That was why this whole tournament was important to him. He's supposed to start teaching there in the fall.

The only thing that frustrated Ashley was that she'd forgotten to write down the e-mail address of the lady from Hollywood. She wasn't able to retrieve the business card before we left.

The ride home was quiet, with most of the team falling asleep as we drove away from Tres Peaks. The only two who didn't sleep were Ashley and Marion. They talked the whole way.

# About the Authors

**Jerry B. Jenkins** (jerryjenkins.com) is the writer of the Left Behind series. He owns the Jerry B. Jenkins Christian Writers Guild, an organization dedicated to mentoring aspiring authors. Former vice president for publishing for the Moody Bible Institute of Chicago, he also served many years as editor of *Moody* magazine and is now Moody's writer-at-large.

His writing has appeared in publications as varied as *Reader's Digest, Parade, Guideposts*, in-flight magazines, and dozens of other periodicals. Jenkins's biographies include books with Billy Graham, Hank Aaron, Bill Gaither, Luis Palau, Walter Payton, Orel Hershiser, and Nolan Ryan, among many others. His books appear regularly on the *New York Times, USA Today, Wall Street Journal,* and *Publishers Weekly* best-seller lists.

Jerry is also the writer of the nationally syndicated sports story comic strip *Gil Thorp,* distributed to newspapers across the United States by Tribune Media Services.

Jerry and his wife, Dianna, live in Colorado and have three grown sons and three grandchildren.

**Chris Fabry** is a writer and broadcaster who lives in Colorado. He has written more than 40 books, including collaboration on the Left Behind: The Kids series.

You may have heard his voice on Focus on the Family, Moody Broadcasting, or Love Worth Finding. He has also written for Adventures in Odyssey and Radio Theatre.

Chris is a graduate of the W. Page Pitt School of Journalism at Marshall University in Huntington, West Virginia. He and his wife, Andrea, have been married 23 years and have nine children, two dogs, and one cat.

# RED ROCK MYSTERIES

The entire series now available: